Shivers in the Dark Anthology of Horror Stories

A Collection of Horror Stories

Debajyoti Gupta, Sushant Thapa, W.J. Manaras

Ukiyoto Publishing

All global publishing rights are held by

Ukiyoto Publishing

Published in 2025

Content Copyright © Debajyoti Gupta, Sushant Thapa, W.J. Manares

ISBN 9789370092730

All rights reserved.

No part of this publication may be reproduced, transmitted, or stored in a retrieval system, in any form by any means, electronic, mechanical, photocopying, recording or otherwise, without the prior permission of the publisher.

The moral rights of the author have been asserted.

This is a work of fiction. Names, characters, businesses, places, events, locales, and incidents are either the products of the author's imagination or used in a fictitious manner. Any resemblance to actual persons, living or dead, or actual events is purely coincidental.

This book is sold subject to the condition that it shall not by way of trade or otherwise, be lent, resold, hired out or otherwise circulated, without the publisher's prior consent, in any form of binding or cover other than that in which it is published.

www.ukiyoto.com

Contents

Burnt Umber
   By W. J. Manares (Philippines) — 1

My House in Las Piñas
   By Alyssum E. Sinclair (Philippines) — 11

The Haunted Shadows of Laagan
   By Shailendrakarki (Nepal) — 22

Behind You
   By Maekawa Kirin (Philippines) — 32

Daily Rations
   By Maekawa Kirin (Philippines) — 45

Ominous Craving
   ShernazWadia (India) — 53

The Small Hours
   By John Drudge (Canada) — 63

Shadow of My Previous Birth
   By TilKumari Sharma (Nepal) — 65

The Open Coffin
   By Sushant Thapa (Nepal) — 71

The Graveyard shift
   By Shiva Neupane, (Nepali-American Writer) — 77

Battle of Powerful witch's Family
   By The Anonymous Hand (Phillipines) — 84

The Bending Bamboo in the Stream

By The Anonymous Hand (Philippines)	107
The Cursed Radio	
By RajendraOjha(Nepal)	118
Belladona's Wrath	
By Ythela Garcia (Philippines)	127
Mystery of the Land of Witchcraft	
By Debajyoti Gupta, India	137
About the Author	*143*

Burnt Umber

By W. J. Manares (Philippines)

Rumors swirled around Mr. Marco Warren's chocolates, tales of their addictive nature and the strange hold they seemed to have over those who indulged in them. But despite the whispers of caution that echoed through the streets, people flocked to Mr. Warren's shop, unable to resist the alluring aroma that wafted from within.

Among the unsuspecting patrons was a young woman named Jeanbelle, whose sweet tooth and insatiable curiosity led her to Mr. Marco Warren's doorstep one evening. The shop was cloaked in shadows, the only light emanating from flickering candles that cast an eerie glow over the gleaming display cases filled with an array of tantalizing treats.

Mr. Warren, a tall and imposing figure cloaked in shadows, greeted Jeanbelle with a toothy smile that sent shivers down her spine. His eyes seemed to pierce her very soul as he offered her a small, glistening chocolate truffle. "Here's your num-nums," offered the chocolatier. Unable to resist, Jeanbelle took a hesitant bite, the rich sweetness exploding on her tongue in a symphony of flavors.

But as the chocolate melted in her mouth, a searing pain ripped through her body, causing her to double over in agony. She watched in horror as tendrils of darkness snaked through her veins, devouring her very essence from the inside out. "Aaaaahhhhhh," her screams echoed through the shop, but Mr. Marco Warren's only watched with a wicked grin as Jeanbelle melted into a puddle of chocolatey goo.

Unbeknownst to Jeanbelle, Mr. Warren was no ordinary chocolatier. He was the demon Beelzebub in disguise, a collector of souls who used his sinister confections to lure unsuspecting victims to their doom. Jeanbelle's essence now joined the countless others that Beelzebub had claimed over the centuries, each soul adding to the twisted magic that infused his chocolates with their dark power.

As Jeanbelle's melted form was collected in a silver goblet by Mr. Marco Warren's twisted minions, the demon chocolatier began to work his dark magic, molding her essence into a new chocolate treat for the next victim to crave and savor. And so the cycle continued, a never-ending nightmare of sin and temptation that kept the people of the town under Mr. Warren's malevolent spell.

As the next unsuspecting patron stepped into Mr. Marco Warren's shop, a glimmer of hope sparked in

Jeanbelle's eyes, for she knew that her journey was far from over.

And so the stage was set for a battle of wills between light and darkness, as Mr. Warren's sinister confections continued to ensnare the souls of the innocent, and Jeanbelle's spirit fought to break free from its chocolatey prison and put an end to the demon chocolatier's reign of terror. But she failed.

As the days passed, more and more people fell victim to Mr. Warren's wicked scheme, their souls consumed by his malevolent chocolates. It wasn't long before whispers of strange occurrences at the chocolate shop began to spread throughout the town.

Mysterious disappearances and unexplained deaths were linked to Mr. Marco Warren's Chocolate Shop, and a sense of unease settled over the once-thriving community. Those who had tasted the chocolates spoke of a darkness that lingered within them, a shadow that seemed to grow stronger with each passing day.

Another victim was a young man named Van, whose love for chocolate had led him to Mr. Warren's shop in search of the perfect treat. But as he bit into a seemingly innocent truffle, he felt a chill creep over him, a sensation of dread that he couldn't shake.

Van sought out others who had experienced similar horrors, forming a secret alliance, the Anti-Chocolate Temptation Society (ACTS) dedicated to uncovering the truth behind Mr. Marco Warren's sinister confections. Together, they delved into the dark underbelly of the town, following whispers and rumors that led them to a terrifying revelation.

Like Jeanbelle, they discovered Mr. Warren's true nature, he was Beelzebub the Demon masquerading as a chocolatier, preying on the souls of the innocent to fuel his dark magic. Determined to stop him, Van and his allies launched a daring raid on the chocolate shop, confronting Beelzebub in a final showdown that would determine the fate of their souls.

The battle raged on, the air thick with the scent of chocolate and the crackling energy of dark magic. Beelzebub's minions fought fiercely to protect their master, but Van and the Anti-Chocolate Temptation Society refused to back down, their determination to free the trapped souls fueling their courage.

Here are 13 ways the Anti-Chocolate Temptation Society defeated the demon chocolatier, Mr. Marco Warren, who is actually Beelzebub:

1. The society created a potion from naturally sweet fruits, which countered the dark magic of chocolate. When they confronted him, they doused him with it, weakening his powers.

2. They unearthed ancient recipes for desserts that could rival chocolate in taste but were made with healthy ingredients. By showcasing the delicious alternatives, they enticed his followers away from his chocolate creations.

3. The society established "chocolate-free zones" in their town, making it a sanctuary for those seeking to resist temptation. This put pressure on Mr. Warren's business, diminishing his influence.

4. Using high-frequency sounds that only demons can hear, they created an audio barrier around Mr. Warren's shop, disrupting his ability to enchant customers with the aroma of chocolate.

5. They organized community potlucks where only non-chocolate desserts were allowed, fostering a sense

of togetherness that diluted demand for Mr. Warren's confections.

6. The society harnessed the power of positive affirmations related to self-control and healthy living, which they broadcasted in town, weakening the will of anyone tempted by chocolate.

7. They launched a series of marketing campaigns featuring sugar-free, gluten-free, and vegan desserts that tempted the populace away from Mr. Warren's chocolate.

8. The society recruited local librarians to spread knowledge about the harmful effects of excessive sugar and the health benefits of a balanced diet, empowering citizens to avoid chocolate.

9. They discovered a way to break Mr. Warren's dark spells by finding a specific ingredient he had used in his chocolate: a rare type of cocoa. Once rendered benign, it stripped him of his magical abilities.

10. The society promoted peer support groups for those struggling with chocolate addiction, providing a platform for sharing success stories and coping strategies.

11. They created subliminal audio recordings that promoted natural foods over chocolate, playing these subtly throughout town to shift public perception subconsciously.

12. The society enlisted local healers to teach workshops on the emotional aspects of food cravings, helping individuals understand and manage their desires for unhealthy treats.

13. In a dramatic showdown, the society gathered their most devoted members to confront Mr. Warren. With an array of healthy snacks and a shared commitment to courageous eating, they overwhelmed him with their resolve, forcing him to retreat back to the underworld.

These combined efforts led to a powerful resistance against temptation, ultimately vanquishing Beelzebub's delicious but dangerous influence in the community.

In the end, Van unleashed a powerful spell that temporarily sealed Beelzebub in the depths of the underworld. The shop itself crumbled into dust, the dark magic that had sustained it dissipating into the ether.

As the dust settled and the city breathed a sigh of relief, rumors began to circulate that Mr. Marco Warren had resurfaced in the Philippines, luring unsuspecting children with his cursed treats. The people whispered of his dark presence, a demonic force that haunted their dreams and lurked in the guise of sweetness and savor of burnt umber.

After almost a decade, Beelzebub had broken the spell that imprisoned him in the depths of the underworld. He then formulated 13 cunning counter-plans for his sweet revenge. He also disguised himself as a charming lady chocolatier who could employ to outsmart Van and the Anti-Chocolate Temptation Society (ACTS) upon his return to the town.

1. Create tantalizing, irresistible chocolates laced with a charm that makes anyone who eats them crave more, enticing ACTS members to abandon their resolutions.

2. Recruit other disguised demons to pose as chocolate lovers, mingling with ACTS members to sow doubt and confusion about their mission.

3. Organize a grand chocolate festival inviting everyone, including ACTS members, to enjoy free samples. The sheer overwhelming quantity and quality of chocolate would weaken their resolve.

4. Introduce a "healthier" chocolate line boasting miraculous benefits and advertise it to attract even the health-conscious members of ACTS, leading them to question their beliefs.

5. Spread false rumors about the negative side effects of completely avoiding chocolate, creating fear and confusion within the community, especially among ACTS members.

6. Develop a batch of chocolates that, when consumed, subtly alter a person's thoughts towards chocolate, convincing them that it's a necessary part of a balanced diet.

7. Host exclusive tasting events that would lure ACTS members in with promises of gourmet chef-created dishes that use chocolate as a base, manipulating them into enjoying and ultimately craving chocolate.

8. Create a guilt-inducing marketing campaign painting ACTS as the "joy-stealers," targeting chocolate lovers with emotional ads about all the happy memories tied to chocolate consumption.

9. Embody the personality of a quintessential, lovable lady chocolatier, using charm and charisma to win over

townspeople and distract them from questioning his true motives.

10. Use illusion magic to create chocolate duplicates of him, spreading confusion about who the real chocolatier is. This would allow him to operate undetected and undermine ACTS from within.

11. Host workshops disguised as wellness events that promote the mental health benefits of chocolate, subtly dismissing ACTS' teachings and redefining their principles.

12. Enlist an army of enchanted critters to spread delicious chocolate around town under the cover of night, promoting nocturnal cravings among unsuspecting residents.

13. Spread misinformation about Van and ACTS, portraying them as extremists who want to ban chocolate completely, thus rallying chocolate lovers against them and securing public support for his sugary schemes.

"Bwahahahaha," Beelzebub's sinister laughter echoing through his newly constructed chocolate shop.

My House in Las Piñas

By Alyssum E. Sinclair (Philippines)

Living in a Christian family, my aunt introduced me to God based on the Bible stories and what God was displeased about in the Bible for simple dos and don'ts as a kid.

My aunt taught me not to lie and not to curse words while she guilt-tripped me, always saying, "God will be sad if you do so." For the cuss words, I have fulfilled them till now, and not to play violent games such as Counter Strike when she found me playing on a PC when I was six years old.

The most memorable word that struck me as a warning was, "A.J., remember it very well that you shouldn't be involved in witchcraft."

I didn't ask her why, but I heeded her word until I broke it when I was in 5th grade.

I remembered it very well at that time, as I was filled with curiosity.

"I wonder why my aunt told me that." I thought.

As a book lover who loves to read novels, I enjoyed collecting physical books.

I started to collect those books when I was in 4th grade, buying them in the bookstore at the Mall of Asia in the Philippines or even at a book fair at my school.

At first, I bought classical novels like The Picture of Dorian Grey and Oliver Twist until it evolved to the most popular novel in my 5th grade, such as The Hunger Games series.

One day, I asked a book seller about what's the most recommended to read, and he told me to follow him until he introduced me to Rick Riordan's works and the Septimus Heap series.

Once more, I remembered what my aunt said—not to be involved in witchcraft.

"Is demi-god included? I think there's nothing wrong with that, and I think it's okay to read witches stories too." I thought carelessly.

Because I was filled with curiosity, I broke my vow to my aunt, and I bought the books that were recommended to me.

Since then, I have loved all of Rick Riordan's works, such as The Percy Jackson series and The Red Pyramid.

As my collection of books grew, there was not enough space in my family's small apartment, so I told my mom to place it in our other house in Las Piñas City, and she agreed.

Our house in La Piñas was three stories high, and no one was living in it as it was quiet too. I considered that house as a vacation house, only visiting during Christmas and New Year.

After I finished reading some books, I sent my collection over to that house.

Little did I know, a lot of supernatural rumors spread in the neighborhood and the supernatural encounters that I experienced.

Whenever we visited that house, I felt the unexplainable overwhelming, heavy presence, and I imagined twenty white ladies were staying in the house.

My heart was pounding erratically in extreme fear as I wanted to leave that house immediately while I was feeling in a state of confusion.

I felt that those twenty white ladies were looking at me, but I hid my insecurities away from my parents and siblings as I felt that they would call me crazy if I confessed.

I decided to keep quiet to myself while I tolerated the strange presence of that house.

As the years grew by, I encountered several supernatural events over at that place.

I remembered one time that after getting food in the kitchen, I placed that food on my plate.

After putting the dishes on my plate, I was walking toward the table. A few meters away, there was a glass sliding door. Instead of my reflection that I was seeing, it was a white lady with a long white gown; her face was hidden by her long black hair on her front, pale skin, and she was barefoot. She was walking to where I was going. I wanted to sit in another place, but I moved forward bravely.

After sitting on the chair, across from me was my little sister.

"Hey, Niks. Did you see what I saw earlier?" I asked her nervously.

My little sister looked at me in confusion and curiosity while she finished chewing her food.

"What is it?" She asked me.

I shook my head and smiled nervously.

"Never mind. I'll tell you later."

I did tell my little sister what I experienced after eating dinner. In return, my little sister told her of her strange encounter on the second floor.

On the second floor, there was a mirror hanging on the wall. What my little sister saw behind a few meters apart was a white lady.

Not only my little sister experienced those things, but also one of our maids.

She remembered that my family and I went outside while my maid was left alone.

She was in the living room, watching TV, until she heard my little brother's childish laughter. At that time, my little brother was a toddler in 2009.

"It must be a doppelganger," one of my maids told me in assumption.

Another one I heard was from the neighborhood. They told one of my family that even though they knew that we were out of the house, they heard loud music begin to play and heard strange noises inside the house.

The most memorable experience I had was hearing a warning. I don't know if it was the Holy Spirit warning me, though.

At that time, when I was going to my parents room on the second floor, I heard a voice in my ear whispering, "Don't sleep on the 3rd floor."

I looked behind my back, and I saw nothing. I was confused and a bit scared.

You see, on the third floor, there were three rooms: a bathroom, my big brother's room, and a shared room between me and my little sister.

Outside of those rooms, that's where my collection of books was.

After hearing that voice, I tried to forget it and move on, but I don't know why because the ghosts sometimes let me know that they were close to me.

For instance, whenever I took a shower in my parent's room, I felt a presence watching over me, and I didn't even go to the third floor because I was afraid of seeing those ghost ladies again.

They only showed up whenever they wanted to, and my fear turned into annoyance, and then I remembered the warning of not sleeping on the 3rd floor.

Curiously, I broke the warning again.

This time, I told one of my maids that I would be sleeping with her in my room since I usually sleep at my parent's room, and there were two beds.

I was awake at midnight, typing on a laptop for my fanfiction.

The electric fan and the air conditioner were ten meters apart from me. Nearby, there was a balcony, and the door was closed.

I saw the curtain nearby in my peripheral vision while I was busy typing on my laptop, and the curtain was moving. I know for a fact that the air conditioner's cold air was not strong enough to move the curtain near me, the electric fan was off, and the balcony's door was closed.

Afraid, I decided to sleep. At exactly three in the morning, I switched off my laptop, prayed, and drifted to dreamland, but my dreamland was not a sweet one because it turned into a bangungut, or a medical term in English, a sudden unexplained nocturnal death syndrome (SUNDS).

I nearly died because of a nightmare.

Inside my nightmare, my body was paralyzed while I couldn't shout for help. I tried to struggle, but it was futile. My heart was beating fast, and my eyes looked at the floating arm, gripping it on my left arm tightly.

I was afraid and confused about my situation. Afraid of what was going on and confused about why, deep inside, I felt pain when the floating arm gripped on me tightly while on the outside, I didn't feel pain at all, and then someone whispered into my mind, "It's a dream."

I woke up dripping in sweat while my heart was pounding fast. On my right side of peripheral vision, I saw my maid sleeping soundlessly. Beside her was a vanity table with a mirror, and I saw the reflection of a white lady.

While my hand was shaking in fear, I opened my laptop, and I saw that six minutes had passed.

On that day, I didn't sleep as I waited for the sun to rise up. After the sun was rising, that's where I started to sleep.

After I experienced a life-and-death situation, I tried to muster my courage to tell my mother.

I was in 6th grade at that time.

One day, when I was in my parent's room while my mother was beside me on the bed I was pretending to type on my laptop, and my confidence swelled inside my chest.

I told my mom the strange encounters I had, but I did not explain to my mother about the bangungut part.

"Are you sure it's not your imagination?" My mother asked me. When I looked at her face, she looked suspicious.

"Yes," I replied while nodding.

Deep inside my mother's chest, I put a seed of doubt. My mother knows that I'm not a liar since I'm very bad at lying.

I thought at that time that my mother didn't believe in me while I felt disappointed, so we kept in awkward silence.

When a year passed by, I became a freshman in high school. I focused on my high school life instead of that house.

I remembered that it was almost the summer of 2012 in Manila. It was after school, and I was excited to read the update of The World God Only Knows manga.

While I was ready to switch on my PC, I was in the living room. Nearby, there was a door where we could enter or leave my parents' apartment. The doorbell rang while I checked on the peephole. It was the mother of my uncle, and she's a pastora (female priest).

I let her in while I closed the door, and we sat on the sofa.

I was looking at her in confusion, wondering why she was here.

She told me, "Did you know that your mother called me?"

"No." I shook my head while I felt nervous.

"You see, your mother called me because of your strange encounter in Las Piñas, so we made an arrangement to bless that house, that was a few days ago." She informed me calmly.

"I called out my two friends or my colleague, and they are pastora like me," she explained.

"We realized that there are many strong spirits living inside that house, and we prayed inside the living room together with your mother," she continued.

"Your mother suddenly got sick because of a spiritual attack, but we fended it off in prayer."

I felt worried after hearing my mother was getting sick, and I felt relieved that she was fine.

"After the prayer in the living room, we began to roam inside the house to open the windows and doors, sprinkling and smearing oils inside the house and proclaiming our Lord Jesus Christ." After hearing this explanation, the pastora further explained why they needed to open the doors and windows. The simple explanation was that the spirits would be let out of the house. The smearing oils on the walls and sprinkling oil were more on not letting the spirits inside the house as a sign of protection, and proclaiming the Lord inside the house would make the spirits flee in the Name of Jesus because they were afraid of Him.

"At first, it was fine on two floors, but as we reached the 3rd floor, one of my friends fainted because of a very strong spirit."

"We ended in victory, and my friend was fine," the pastora assured me.

"We discovered why a lot of spirits lived in that house. Did you know that we Christians aren't allowed to put gargoyles and statues in the household?"She started to explain the spiritual side, and I shook my head as my answer while I quietly listened. Truthfully, at that time, I didn't know where it was going, but I was fascinated.

"You see, when we have those images or statues, spirits can live inside those items, and it will end up having an *opengate* inside people's houses. They now have the authority to destroy the family's daily lives," she continued. Thinking back on what the pastora said in the past, I remembered one of the ten commandments in the bible, "You shall not make idols." in Exodus 20:4.

"Inside that house, there were a few vases that had spirits living within, but the most powerful one was the books of the third floor, so we destroyed it outside your home at Las Piñas by breaking off the vases and burning the books." She recounted that after destroying those things, they heard a loud scream from the burning books until they quieted down when the books turned into ashes. She told me that she couldn't sell the books because a powerful spirit lived within. For the added bonus of passing some of her knowledge to me, she warned me to buy items carefully since some people didn't know that those items that they brought home had curses.

The pastora asked me if there were witches' stories in those books, and I said yes.

After hearing my answer, she told me the hierarchy of hell. Witches were one of the top five in the hierarchy, while dragons were the second highest. Since it has been a decade since the pastora told me that, I can't remember the rest.

All this time after the pastora informed me about that event, I was crying in relief and felt my weight lifted on my shoulder, and I was in an emotional mess.

I'm glad that my mother believed in me and called the three pastoras for help. When the pastora told me to bring my mom and my siblings in the living room to pray, I did what she ordered me to.

During her prayers, I closed my eyes, and I suddenly imagined a ball of light roaming in the living room. I thought it was the Holy Spirit because I felt peace and joy within.

After the pastora's prayer, she went home while I felt emotionally drained.

I decided to sleep at seven in the evening, and then I saw a vision.

I saw a painting of angels and demons fighting inside that house, and the angels were winning. I knew immediately that Jesus was comforting me through a vision, and I felt relief and thankfulness to Him.

Since then, I never felt scared of going to my house in Las Piñas, for I know that our Lord protected that house.

The Haunted Shadows of Laagan

By Shailendrakarki (Nepal)

In the narrow alleys of Laagan, Kathmandu, nestled among the old brick houses and towering temples, lived a boy named Rohan. He was a shy and introverted child, always keeping to himself, his presence as quiet as a whisper. His days at school were spent in the farthest corner of the classroom, where he would doodle in his notebook, escaping into a world of wild imagination. He rarely spoke, and when he did, his voice was so soft that it often went unheard.

Rohan loved watching the other children play, but he never joined them. One late afternoon, as the sun dipped behind the rooftops, casting long shadows across the dusty playground, Rohan sat on the edge, his eyes following the children as they played cricket. The shouts and laughter filled the air, but Rohan felt distant, like an observer from another world. As he sat there lost in thought, a cricket ball suddenly flew toward him, too fast for him to react. It struck him on the head with a sharp thud, and everything went black.

When Rohan awoke, he was lying on a wooden cot in his family's dimly lit room. The walls were adorned with old photographs and Newari handicrafts, and the scent of incense lingered in the air. His head throbbed with pain, and as he blinked his eyes open, he noticed something strange. Standing at the foot of his bed was a figure—a ghostly apparition with translucent skin, its face twisted in a perpetual scowl.

Rohan's heart raced as the ghost moved closer, but when he tried to scream, no sound escaped his lips. The ghost was terrifying, but there was something oddly familiar about it. As he stared into its hollow eyes, he realized it bore a striking resemblance to the bullies at school who had always intimidated him. This ghost, he would later name "*Wangukhycha*", had a ghastly green hue and seemed to emit an aura of anger and frustration.

The encounter left Rohan trembling with fear, but that was only the beginning. Over the next few days, more ghosts began to appear. There was "*Kichakhycha*", a shadowy figure with a deep indigo shade, who always loomed behind Rohan, whispering fears of failure and self-doubt into his ears. Then came "*Hangukhycha*", a crimson-red ghost with sharp features and fiery eyes, representing his hidden anger and resentment that he had never dared to express.

At first, Rohan was petrified. He couldn't understand why these ghosts haunted him, and he had no one to turn to. His shyness made it impossible for him to share his experiences with his parents or teachers. He started to avoid everyone even more, isolating himself in his room, where the ghosts would appear every night. They taunted him, reminding him of his weaknesses, playing tricks on his mind. The temperature in his room would suddenly drop, books would fall off shelves, and eerie whispers filled the silence. He began to lose sleep, and his grades started to suffer. The cheerful boy who once found solace in his imagination now dreaded the darkness of his own mind.

But as weeks passed, something began to change. Rohan noticed that the ghosts weren't just tormenting him—they were trying to communicate. He started to listen to them, really listen, and in their cryptic messages, he began to see a reflection of his own inner turmoil. "Wangukhycha" was the embodiment of his fear of confrontation, "Kichakhycha" his crippling self-doubt, and "Hangukhycha" his unexpressed anger.

One evening, as Rohan sat alone in his room, he found the courage to speak to them. "Why are you here?" he asked, his voice trembling. The ghosts didn't respond with words, but their expressions softened, and Rohan could feel their intensity lessen. Slowly, he began to realize that they were not here to harm him, but to help him understand the emotions he had buried deep inside.

He decided to face them one by one. With "Wangukhycha", Rohan started standing up for himself, first in small ways—by raising his hand in class, by asking questions, by refusing to be pushed around by his peers. The more he did this, the weaker "Wangukhycha" became, until one day, the green ghost faded away, leaving behind a sense of calm that Rohan had never known.

With "Kichakhycha", Rohan confronted his fears of failure. He began to participate more in class, taking on challenges even if they scared him. The indigo shadow gradually shrank, its whispers turning into words of encouragement rather than doubt.

"Hangukhycha" was the hardest to deal with. Rohan had always bottled up his anger, fearing that expressing it would make him a bad person. But with the help of the other ghosts, he learned that it was okay to feel anger, as long as he channeled it constructively. He started journaling his feelings, pouring out his frustrations on paper. Slowly, the red ghost too began to diminish, its fiery eyes softening as Rohan learned to manage his emotions.

The transformation in Rohan was remarkable. The boy who had once been too afraid to speak now walked with a quiet confidence. He started to make friends, and his teachers noticed a change in his demeanor. He was no longer the shy boy who hid in the corner but a young man who faced his fears head-on.

The ghosts, once terrifying, became his guides. They no longer haunted him but stayed as silent companions, a reminder of the journey he had undertaken. Rohan knew they would always be a part of him, but they no longer controlled his life. Instead, they were symbols of his strength, his resilience, and his ability to overcome the darkest parts of himself.

As Rohan stood on the balcony of his home in Laagan, overlooking the narrow streets of Kathmandu, he felt a sense of peace. The city was alive with the sounds of evening prayers, the ringing of temple bells, and the distant cacophony of bazaar life. And in the midst of it all, Rohan had found his voice, his courage, and his place in the world.

The shadows in his room no longer frightened him, for he knew that the real ghosts were the ones we carry within us, and that the only way to banish them was to confront them, understand them, and ultimately, to embrace them.

As the months passed, Rohan's life in Laagan, Kathmandu, continued to evolve. The once timid boy had grown into someone who could face his fears, and the ghosts that had haunted him became quieter, more subdued. However, they never completely disappeared. Instead, they lingered like old friends, watching over him, their presence a reminder of the journey they had shared.

Rohan's newfound confidence began to ripple through his life in unexpected ways. He started engaging more in school, not just academically but also socially. He joined a small group of students who shared his interest in storytelling and art. Together, they would sit under the ancient banyan tree near the temple and create stories filled with heroes and mythical creatures. For the first time, Rohan wasn't afraid to share his ideas, and his stories quickly became the most popular in the group. The other children admired his imagination and the way he could weave tales that felt as real as the world around them.

One afternoon, as the group gathered under the banyan tree, a peculiar chill filled the air. The sky, once bright and clear, darkened with clouds that seemed to roll in from nowhere. The children looked up, confused, as a cold breeze rustled the leaves above them. Rohan felt a familiar sensation—a prickling at the back of his neck, a whisper in the air. The ghosts were near.

But this time, they weren't alone.

From the shadows of the banyan tree emerged a new figure, one that Rohan had never seen before. This ghost was different from the others, more menacing, with a form that shifted and writhed like a mass of black smoke. Its eyes were two burning coals, and its presence filled Rohan with a deep, bone-chilling dread. The other children couldn't see the ghost, but they could feel something was wrong. They huddled closer together, glancing nervously at Rohan, who was staring at the ghost with wide eyes.

The ghost hovered before Rohan, its smoky tendrils reaching out toward him. "Who are you?" Rohan asked, his voice trembling. The ghost didn't reply in words, but a deep, guttural sound rumbled from within it, filling the air with an oppressive weight.

Rohan's old ghosts—"Wangukhycha", "Kichakhycha", and "Hangukhycha"—appeared beside him, their forms flickering like candle flames in a strong wind. They were smaller now, their colors muted, but they stood between Rohan and the new ghost, as if trying to protect him. Rohan could feel their fear, and it unnerved him. This new entity was something they couldn't easily confront.

As the new ghost loomed closer, Rohan began to understand. This ghost wasn't born from his own emotions like the others; it was something darker, something that fed on fear and despair. It was "*Bhayankarkhycha*", a manifestation of the collective fears of the people around him—the fears of the unknown, of change, of dissatisfaction and envy. It was the fear that gripped entire communities, passed down through generations, lingering in the shadows of Kathmandu's ancient narrow streets.

Rohan knew he couldn't face "Bhayankarkhycha" alone. The ghost was too powerful, too overwhelming. He needed help. And so, for the first time, Rohan turned to the friends he had made. "There's something here," he said, his voice steady despite the fear gnawing at his insides. "I need your help to face it."

The other children looked at him, confused and scared, but Rohan's calmness gave them strength. They didn't understand what was happening, but they trusted him. Together, they held hands, forming a circle around Rohan. They closed their eyes, following Rohan's lead, and began to think of the things that made them strong—their families, their dreams, the warmth of their homes, and the love that connected them.

As they focused on these positive thoughts, Rohan felt a shift in the air. The oppressive weight of "Bhayankarkhycha" began to lift, replaced by a warmth that spread through their circle. The ghost hesitated, its form flickering, its power waning in the face of their collective strength. Rohan's old ghosts stood taller, their colors brightening as they fed off the positive energy.

And then, in a final act of courage, Rohan stepped forward, facing "Bhayankarkhycha" directly. "You don't control me," he said, his voice firm. "We all have fears, but they don't define us. You can't take away what makes us strong."

With those words, "Bhayankarkhycha" let out a low, mournful wail, its form dissolving into the air like smoke on the wind. The sky began to clear, and the warmth of the sun broke through the clouds, bathing the children in light. The chill in the air disappeared, and the oppressive feeling lifted, replaced by a sense of peace and relief.

The other children opened their eyes, smiling at each other, unaware of the battle they had just won but feeling the weight of fear lift from their hearts. They laughed, the sound filling the air with life and joy. Rohan stood in the center of the circle, smiling softly, his heart light. He knew that "Bhayankarkhycha" might return one day, but he also knew that he wasn't alone. He had his friends, and together, they were stronger than any fear.

As the evening sun set over Kathmandu, casting a golden glow over the ancient city, Rohan felt a deep sense of calmness. The ghosts, his old companions, faded back into the shadows, their presence no longer needed but always there, watching over him. He had faced the darkness within and beyond, and had emerged stronger, not just for himself, but for those around him.

In his journey of fight in fear and isolations Rohan was ready for whatever lay ahead. He had learned that bravery wasn't the absence of fear, but the courage to face it head-on. And as he walked home through the winding streets of Laagan, the ghosts of his past walked with him, silent but proud, guiding him toward a future he could now face without fear.

Behind You

By Maekawa Kirin (Philippines)

Never let the light in.

These were the sole words I could remember my father by.

The point at which these *happenings* occurred was unclear, and memories of my earlier childhood had grown cloudier by the day. But one thing was continually in my mind—a thought perpetually imprinted in everyone's head.

We were all living in constant fear of the *Things from the light*.

I vividly remember playing around with my buddies outside, hopping inside bushes to conceal ourselves from the seeker, seeing whose stone could skip the most on the nearby river, and flinging our slippers at tin cans to fight over who was the most accurate. Those were the days I always look back to amidst my dull life of today. It was then that I could roam freely without the need to constantly look behind me, fearful of *something* creeping out from behind. Those moments were the best, and it was then that I felt alive the most, but those days were long gone. Now, I... no, *everyone* was caged inside their homes, hiding from the *Things from the light*.

I awoke this morning like usual—enveloped by absolute darkness. One would usually stretch for a bit, scroll through social media, turn on the lights, fix their bed, and then get on with their day. On the other hand, I simply stretched and then thought about what I could do to get through this day, the next day, the day after that, the next week, and then, for God knows how many more days after. Fear has always been in my mind, but boredom is synonymous with it. For one, I do not have a single clue on what we should be afraid of. I've heard numerous stories floating by about the *Things from the light*, them being most active during the day, going outside is equal to a death sentence, and even instances of people being attacked in their own homes—the only place everyone hoped would be their haven away from these *creatures*—but no. Nowhere is safe. All these accounts, and yet I'm not precisely sure what these *things* actually appear like or how dangerous of a threat they brought.

I then left my room without batting an eye on how cluttered my bed was. There was no point in doing those kinds of things. Aesthetic appeal no longer mattered since how could one appreciate the beauty of organized objects when there was no light to allow for scrutiny? The only standard now is that you recall where the things you use daily are.

My mother's whispers could be heard as I got to our living room. It was a scenery I saw day-to-day—my mother, alone in the dark, surrounded by heavily boarded-up windows and barricading furniture.

"Morning, Mom. Who are you talking to?"

"Hey there, sweetie. It's your nephew from the States. They're just checking if we're alright. Go and eat up. It's on the table. I already ate, so go on without me."

"Lies," I muttered under my breath. I then ate breakfast silently, observing the dark silhouette of my mother sitting by the telephone stand.

After the appearance of the *Things from the light,* any form of lumination, be it from the sun or even those from the slim LED screens of smartphones, was deemed severely dangerous, enough for a city-wide ban. I'm uncertain if this phenomenon has reached other places due to our broken radio and not having contact with other people besides those in our communities. The use of a television was, of course, out of the question. The only way to communicate was through landlines and handwritten letters—though the latter was barely used due to visibility and safety issues.

I examined my mother's sickly frame, wishing that she would get better eventually. I clasped my hands together and prayed for it to happen.

A sudden ring from the landline shocked my mother back to her senses, almost dropping the telephone on the floor as she strived to keep her shaking hands at bay.

"H-Hello. Who is it…?"

The voice from the other end was inaudible to me, but the reactions on my mother's face were enough for me to conclude their message.

As the call continued, I could observe how my mother stood erect in a flash, leaned on the wall on her back, scratched her head, and then slowly lost power in her legs, plunging to the floor with the telephone continuously resonating a flat tone, indicating that the call had already come to an end.

Tears began to trickle from her eyes as she attempted to wipe them away, but it was foolish in the sense that one could not block a leak with mere tape, for it would succumb to its pressure. She was a mess, and I knew this more than her.

"Mom, what's wrong?" I questioned, hoping for her to enlighten me with their conversation. I knew that keeping things in would only worsen it, so I opened a way for her to let it all out.

"It's Nathalie... S-She's... g-gone..." The flow of her tears then reached its apex.

I embraced her, repeatedly whispering, "It will be alright, Mom," until she eventually calmed down. This scene wasn't new to me. It's an exact one-to-one of the events from last week, the week before, and the month before. Every time terrible news reached my mother's ear, it was always up to me to keep her sane.

From the words of another of my mother's friends, Nathalie, one of her closest companions from college who lived just by the riverbank, had been attacked by the *Things from the light*. The events all happened before the sun of today had risen. In the quiet night, due to increasingly poor eyesight and fear for her safety, Nathalie had done the taboo. She lit a candle to aid in traversing the steep stairs of their home, more afraid of falling to her death rather than the dangers of what might come from a single ember. All was well as she took step after step. To her, enough haste would make it so the *creatures* wouldn't have enough time to notice her. But all it took was a single moment. The crackle of the flame, the swaying of the light, the sweat sliding down her frigid cheeks, and then... a movement in her peripheral.

It was behind her.

She turned around, but it was too late! *The Thing from the light* was already there, looming behind her like a dark curtain. She couldn't see the *creature* in full—no one had ever done it in the past. All reports only state that they had caught a glimpse of the *things* before they shifted with utmost speeds, like a dog chasing its own tail—it was almost impossible to witness it in the act.

Then, as everyone feared, *it* had attacked. The *creature* reportedly shoved Nathalie down the stairs, and the fall was so abrupt that she had not a single second to scream out in terror. Her head had bashed on a step on the stairs, cracking her skull open and sending her down like a hay bale tumbling down a hill and finally crashing on the ground, alone, cold, unmoving, dead...

The candle came after her and was extinguished by the fall.

The *creature* was no longer there.

It was cruel, it was unjust, it was unfair. To have your life taken away from you in a single moment, a mere instance of wanting to enjoy life's daily necessity—light, taking away our desires, our needs, our rights…

Life had already become bleak with the monotonous darkness. But the frequent deaths made it a living hell.

I stroked my mother's hair, calming her down more and more. It was now at a point where her hands shook no longer, but the ugliness in her expression had yet to vanish.

My poor mother…

It wasn't always like this. I still remember the times when her face could form a smile despite the dangers plaguing our surroundings. Moments where sharing jokes was the primary way for us to waste the day away. Times I hold dear in my heart, yet… gone… gone, gone, gone… It had vanished like the light, with it all stemming from the loss of our beloved father.

I have not much of a recollection of him. All I remember is that a fuse had clicked in his head one day, and he turned into a skeptic—one who questioned the existence of the *Things from the light*. He had attempted to force the barricades out from the entrance many times. Yet, it was because of my mother that he got to live another day, persuading him to postpone his plans for exploration. But the inevitable was soon to happen.

Being deprived of the light, with the addition of the desire to know more—a combination that could lead to death, and it undoubtedly did for him. As the night echoed its eerie silence, my father had sneaked out and hadn't returned until the flash of daylight, but by then, it was already too late. We woke up from sudden screaming and saw how my father was hunched over the makeshift barricade of furniture, which looked newly arranged, indicating that they were once taken down and placed back without much thought, only prioritizing that the gaps were completely filled. He was frozen, hugging his knees and muttering repeatedly, "It's behind me, it's behind me, it's behind me…"

We tried the best we could to nurse him back to health, but not a single ounce of food entered his stomach, nor a drop of water nourished his dried skin. It was like he hadn't slept a minute despite being on his bed all day, unmoving, eyes open wide, hands shaking, muttering, "It's behind me, it's behind me, it's behind me…"

We couldn't speak to him, nor could he talk back to us. He was no longer the father I loved.

The muttering had finally ceased one evening, yet his condition hadn't improved. Mother placed a knife on his bedside table just for him to feel more secure from having a mode of defense, but we would later discover that this would be her gravest mistake.

I was about to close the door to my father's room when suddenly, he turned to look at me.

"Never let the light in," he whispered in a hoarse breath.

I ignored his message. "Goodnight, Dad," I said as I left him in the dark, alone, weak, and afraid.

The day after that, I and my mother awoke to yet another bleak day, but my father, for once, was asleep... *forever*.

We found him in his same position, straight like a log, eyes wide open... a knife stuck to his chest. It had pierced his hand first before plunging into the depths of his heart, maybe thinking that the hand on his chest was from the *Things from the light*.

We had lost my father once to them, and now we lost him again, this time permanently...

To this day, my mother blamed herself for my father's death. Any source of light had been heavily patched up and disposed of, even going as far as taking all the lightbulbs out of their sockets and stashing them all in a drawer, never to see the light of day or any light for that matter.

The same could be said with my father's body. Without access to a proper burial ground, due to obvious reasons, we had laid him to rest in the one place he felt at home—his own room, which was now closed off. Even now, I can smell the stench of whatever was left inside, seeping through the gaps of the door.

"What's for lunch, Mom?"

"I haven't checked, sweetie. Scan the fridge and tell me what you'd like," Mother said as she held the telephone to her ear.

I sighed, knowing that even if it was a real call or not, nothing good could come from it.

I placed my hands together again and prayed.

Please get better, Mom.

I peeked inside the fridge and noticed we were running out of rations. The few ways anyone could stock up on food is if they were to grow some sort of plant that didn't require sunlight or order groceries through the landline. No one questioned how people could deliver packages around. All we know is that whenever there's knocking on the door, it's *them*. We would blindfold ourselves as we took out parts of the barricade. Our door had this small doggy door on the bottom and was the perfect size for sliding boxes inside. Mother would stick her arms outside—the most vulnerable instant, but it was a necessary risk, or else we'd starve. Then, upon feeling a solid figure, she'd pull it in. That's how we get food monthly, and the way of cooking was, of course, through pressure and rice cookers, with their LED indicators taken out.

"Y-You were attacked?!" Mother exclaimed through the phone. "B-But all your uncle did was light a cigarette, r-right?"

I didn't want to chime in on their conversation. I knew too well that either someone was injured or had perished from being attacked by the *Things from the light*. Instead, I focused on picking out ingredients and pondering whether I could prepare our meal myself to console my mother if she ever heard gossip about other unfortunate news.

Upon taking out a plastic container filled with chops of meat, I saw what appeared to be a wall of tape covering the edge of the fridge on the side of the hinge.

"What's this?" I muttered to myself.

Because this was the only time I've seen the fridge nearing empty, I've only noticed this odd detail now. It was like someone had emptied an entire roll of tape trying to fix a crack or something.

I don't know whether it was curiosity, boredom, or a mix of both, but I slowly peeled away at it, unveiling what was hidden behind it piece after piece.

"Sweetie, are you... t-there?" I could hear my mother's sniffles.

Just as I had predicted.

I ignored her for a second. I could now clearly see something pushed down by the tape, like a button perhaps. I peeled more and more until...

Light appeared.

The sudden flash of the fridge blinded me and made me cover my eyes. In those moments, an attack from the *Things from the light* didn't pop up in my head.

Instead, I was dazzled by the bright scenery, as if I had fulfilled a goal and had reached a point of enlightenment. It was amazing.

"Behind you!" my mom yelled out.

I turned to look and was met with a glimpse of... the *thing*. No words could escape my mouth as I finally bore witness to it. I felt no fear nor danger in its form. And yet... I sensed something was odd—without a doubt, something was wrong with the *creature*. It's like there was a thought in my head that wanted to resurface but was blocked off by something. All I could process was that the *creature* was indeed huge.

I was looking behind me, but somehow, I knew that my mom was hurling herself towards me from my side, trying to reach and push me away from the *Things from the light*. The moment I felt her touch, everything went black...

I woke up alone, cold, and troubled.

"Mom... What happened?" I muttered, but no one answered back.

Suddenly, I felt as if my head was being ripped open, repeatedly being bashed in by something.

I tried to bottle up the pain. It was just a headache, yet it wasn't dissipating, not in the slightest.

Then I remembered the *creature*—the *Things from the light*.

"Those aren't monsters..." I muttered, unaware of what my tongue had slipped out. Then, suddenly, something clicked in my head, and the pain had vanished.

A moment of silence passed by as I formed a thought in my head—one that would turn everything I... no—everything that everyone knew upside down.

Before my mom had shoved me away, I was staring at *it*—the very creature everyone feared, the entity that had caused numerous deaths, the one who made my mother the way she was.

I was staring at... *myself.*

It was dark, it was large, it occupied the entirety of the wall, and it had a human-like silhouette. Then, as my mom was about to push me, another of these *things* emerged, looking like hands reaching out from the void of the darkness.

But these weren't *monsters*.

All the *attacks* that occurred weren't from the work of a deadly entity. There was no way something could suddenly come from a flash of light and strike you instantly. Those were all made up—a result of our imagination, a delusion from something molding our perceptions to fear what is not there.

Somehow... or something... had brainwashed everyone to lose the concept of *it*.

Never let the light in.

I recalled my father's words.

He's wrong, my mom's wrong, they're wrong—everyone is wrong!

They need to know the truth. That everything is all a lie.

I stood up with my fist clenched and braved the bleak darkness once more. This time, yearning for the light.

There was no need to be afraid… There was no need to hide… The *Things from the light* weren't real. The truth behind them is that all this time, they were our…

Shadows…

It was now up to me to enlighten this hell with the truth.

To return to what was once normal.

It's time to leave these fears *behind us*.

I need to let the light in.

Daily Rations

By Maekawa Kirin (Philippines)

I exhaled a sigh of relief as I tucked the canned meat into my satchel.

Looks like we'll make it through this month.

It had been three years since the apocalypse had begun. Out of nowhere, monsters had invaded the earth and slaughtered all living beings indiscriminately. The purpose behind those monsters doing all these horrid things remains unknown, but it's not hard to imagine they are scheming world domination—through mass genocide, that is. All of humanity retreated into the shadows, surrendering most of the surface, including farmlands and water sources, in the hands of those creatures. As fewer and fewer people survived the attacks, so did our supplies.

My current settlement was in an underground bunker built near the foot of the mountain surrounded by a forest. We were a community of originally fifty families but now dwindled to only twenty after numerous failed expeditions where the volunteers never came back, coupled with disease and starvation from the lack of clean water and food.

My brother, who turned ten a week ago, had contracted a disease. There were no doctors on board, so we could only hope that he'd get better by eating more, but our daily rations of potatoes and salty dirt-filtered water weren't cutting it. We needed something better—enough to nurture our bodies and not just satisfy our stomachs temporarily—and fast.

I strapped my satchel back on my shoulder as I peeked from a broken window. Degraded buildings, snapped street lights, abandoned cars—destruction had rained like an incessant storm to which the landscape before me was the outcome. A deep breath came out of me before I creaked open the door and ran out on my tiptoes, trying to be as silent as a mouse and using the scattered cars as cover.

I had to be careful. There was no knowing when a monster might spring forth from the shadows to strike me down like the others. In actuality, I have no clue what those monsters are capable of or what they even look like. All the news we've gotten described them as humanoid in shape and nothing more. I volunteered for a ration run because no one else had the balls to go after our community chief, who had volunteered before me, didn't return after the agreed one-week recall time. I had to do it. I couldn't just leave my brother dying of a mere disease. The only death that I would accept was perishing to those creatures, but not before I give them a piece of my mind—my anger, my soul—everything I've got. For me, it's most noble to die fighting.

I slithered into an alleyway and emerged on the other end, welcomed by the stench of rotting meat and the visual chaos of the street that looked to have been run over by a tornado of rubbish. It was one of those impoverished areas of the city—mostly sections where squatters and those who have nowhere to go tend to congregate. People here lived a desperate existence even before those monsters ravaged everything, but now that it has turned into a ghost town, it's beyond depressing.

The ground felt like a minefield as I avoided plastic wrappers and tin cans crunching beneath my feet, though I took my time scrutinizing all and sundry to gather more rations before returning to my bunker. Every potato chip and tiny drop of soda counts.

Upon reaching another tight alleyway, violent thuds and clacking echoed from the other side.

Is it them?

I gulped nervously and drew a deep breath as if trying to gather courage. I got down low and held my six-shooter at the ready, loading a bullet and cocking the hammer. All left was to aim, pull back my index, and give those monsters a taste of lead.

I crouched closer and closer to the sound. Just steps away, I saw garbage being flung to the ground and the wall opposite of it, banging, rebounding, and clacking before it settled, further adding filth to the alley.

I peeked over and saw the figure. It was a tall human-shaped being that wore a tattered black trench coat, ripped jeans, and topped off with a tan tweed golf cap. It stood facing away from me and looked to be sifting through a garbage can. As much as it seemed human, there was no telling if it was one.

"Don't move!" I ordered as I pointed my gun at it.

The figure shuddered, toppling over the garbage can before raising its hands in compliance.

"I... I-I'm not a threat," the voice of a man in his forties replied.

"Turn around."

He did as he was told and we made eye contact afterward. It was indeed a man, and looked to be deprived of sleep—his face garnished with bags under bags and had an unkempt mustache and beard reaching to the middle of his chest.

"Are you human," I asked him whilst pointing my gun.

He nodded repeatedly, fearing to look at anything other than the barrel of my six-shooter.

"I don't know what you want, b-but I have food if that's what you need," the man spoke out while his jaw jittered.

I holstered my gun. Looks like he's on the clear.

The man led me across alleyways and cityscapes until we reached the city's border. His house was lined on the edge of a forest and beyond it sounded like a flowing river. It was a less-than-ideal house, mainly constructed of scraped wood hammered together, fenced with stacked car tires to keep it sturdy, roofed by one large sheet of metal held down by rocks, and decorated with vines and other flora that made it look like the forest was slowly reclaiming it.

A woman waited by the door, dressed in a black shirt, thigh-high brown shorts, and a long, flowing, dirt-colored coat. Her face beamed as she saw us approach.

They welcomed me into their home. Inside was what you'd expect: broken furniture, holed flooring, the scent of rust, makeshift appliances, and a lone light that flickered every few seconds.

The man introduced the woman as his wife, and sat in a wheelchair facing a table was their son. Both his legs and his left arm were missing and most of his body was covered in bandages, with some parts still moist from red stains. He looked to be unable to speak from the bandages covering his mouth and one of his eyes was also patched up. If you were to pull out large patches of weeds randomly in a greenfield, it would perfectly describe the boy's hair. His single eye didn't move as we entered, seeming like he didn't care about anything anymore. All his attention was on the boarded-up window with only specks of light shining through. The boy looked sad, and even I grew sad the more I looked at him—if I were to lose most of my limbs then of course I'd give up on life. At the very least, he's still holding on.

I clenched my fist. *Those monsters will definitely pay!* Injuries of that caliber could only result from an attack by those monsters.

The wife sat me down at the front of the table, and after a few minutes of tinkering in the kitchen, she served me a small meat patty the size of a clenched fist.

"I can't accept this now that I know your situation," I said as I pushed the plate away, but then she pulled it back.

"Don't worry about it. Our daily rations have just arrived. We have plenty to go around."

I took a gulp of guilt before taking the first bite. It was absolutely delicious—mouthwatering even. The meat crumbled with just a slight chew, releasing its fatty oils and enveloping the entirety of my tongue. Some of its juices even seeped out of my mouth and covered my lips, its scent wafting up my nostrils. Don't even get me started about the taste. I took bite after bite and wished it would never end with each mouthful.

"Aren't you all gonna join me?" I asked as I chewed my recent bite.

"It's fine, we just ate. Go and enjoy yourself until it lasts," answered the father. Both of them then went outside and announced, "We'll just be getting some firewood for tonight. Wait for us before you go."

"Sure, and also, thank you!" I exclaimed before they could shut the door, almost forgetting to thank their hospitality.

No matter how many times its flavor slams down on my taste buds, the ecstasy never leaves. I hadn't had meat in a while, and my mouth was already dripping when I saw that canned meat back while I was looting.

Upon my penultimate bite, the boy had moved his attention from the window and was now on me. He stared me in the eyes and made an even sadder expression—the side of his lone eyebrow drooping down as a tear fell across his wrapped cheek.

He rocked his body forward and back repeatedly until suddenly, he fell out of his wheelchair. I rushed to him as he tried to crawl with his single arm.

"Are you stupid, what are you doing?!" I exclaimed.

"...ry," the boy groaned with his raspy voice. It was the only syllable I could understand.

"Is something wrong? Did you hurt yourself?"

With his bandaged arm, he twitched his middle finger, which was the only finger left in his hand, and pointed to his mouth as if telling me to get closer and listen.

I leaned over some more.

"Hu... ry..."

"Hurry?" I translated from his groans.

"...out."

"A bit louder," I asked, his mouth kissing my ear at this point.

"Get…" The boy took a deep, raspy breath. "…out."

"Get… out. Get out?" I put the boy's words together. "Hurry, get out?"

He closed his eye and slowly nodded, giving me confirmation. I felt a chill creep up my neck as I realized what was happening. I eyed the boy from the top down and then remembered the meat I ate.

"It can't be!" My finger jittered as the thought formed in my mind. "I need to get out of here!"

"And who's leaving?" a voice surprised me from behind. Before I could turn, the frightened expression on the boy's eye was clearly visible. He struggled, trying to crawl away by wiggling his body as if behind me was the most horrifying monster he'd ever seen.

I slowly turned my head around.

It was them.

"You can't go now of all times," said the man in a playful tone as he held a hatchet high in the air.

The woman giggled and smiled in the creepiest way that made my entirety shake. "It will be a shame if we lose our daily rations now."

Ominous Craving

ShernazWadia (India)

Echoes of a long-suppressed memory were deafening in the void of Jivi's mind. They stripped off the rind of her superficially calm exterior to reveal the tyranny of a bleeding conscience.

The accordion-pleated carpet of night unfolded its magic — kerosene lamps casted long shadows in both mud huts and brick houses; a distant hum of tree-crickets softly strummed the air. Occasionally stray dogs barked, were shooed away and then the night was still. Only the banyan tree seemed to whisper, "come here, I have many a tale to tell you...scary, scandalous, uncanny and of noble deeds". Its knotted roots swung and creaked chillingly.

In the dreadful dark her relentless memory began to unreel bitter moments tainted with confusion and remorse. Every time her mind grasped for redemption there was only an abyss of self-reproach. The reel played on.

Caught back to a moonless, torrid night. The dying embers of a funeral pyre appeared sinister on the burning ghat. A bat screeched somewhere, disquieting Jivi. Strange shadows flitted on the almost invisible river. Across on the other bank, a dog wailed, making her flesh crawl. Involuntarily her hand reached out to Kali's. Kali patted it reassuringly and whispered, "Don't worry. You are on the threshold of realizing your dream." Jivi wasn't sure; perspiration bristled on her eyelashes, ran down her temples. Her hands were clammy, her mouth and throat went dry; her heart palpitated wildly. She wanted to flee this place where even the dead did not walk at night.

A rustle in the bushes to her left as a figure emerged from the trees and walked towards them. Jivi was petrified but Kali stood up with alacrity and dragged Jivi towards the looming figure, forcing her to bow.

"Jai BholeNath. Follow me" growled the sadhu, loud enough for only their ears.

Jivi seemed to have grown roots. An excited and impatient Kali pushed her ahead fiercely; they were soon in front of another pyre that greedily devoured someone's lifeless flesh. The sadhu's dark face haloed by matted hair and an unkempt dirty beard were clearly visible now. He wore only a loin cloth with ash smeared over his body. The garland of bones adorning his thick neck spooked Jivi. He nodded at Kali and then turned a piercing gaze on Jivi. She felt impaled by the stealthy, unflinching eyes of a fiendish reptile.

"Swamiji, this is Jivi. She has been married for eight years but has no issues."

"You have come to the right place", he snorted. His thin lips parted, in a grimace, revealing stained teeth. "Come close to this fire, to my right."

Paralysed as she was, Jivi heard a strange voice pleading distantly, "I will do whatever you say. Just grant me this boon."

"Have you brought what I had asked for?" He looked at Kali.

"Yes, swamiji. Jivi give your bundle to him."

Again like an automaton, Jivi handed over the bundle. She had stolen five thousand rupees in cash plus gold jewelry from her unsuspecting family. She had also brought along a coconut, a packet of incense sticks and some flowers. The sadhu signaled that she should put it all between them.

Chanting indecipherable mantras he sprinkled some powder onto the pyre, which leapt with a splintering crackle into bluish-green tongues. He kept pulling the powder and whatever else he threw into the fire, from a well-polished human skull. Lulled into the realm of possibility, she was ready to go through anything. The intensity of the incantations rose with the stinging smoke. Without a pause the sadhu picked up the coconut and flowers and tossed them into the flames. Then he tied an amulet on her arm and sprinkled her hair and shoulders with ash, a frightening gleam in his eyes. He began to chant faster and with renewed ferocity.

Jivi was hynotised. She began to sway dangerously. Rising she began a bizarre dance around the pyre, twirling and croaking, loosened hair flying around her like small dragons from some netherworld.

When she awoke the next morning, she felt groggy. There was a dull ache in her body. She looked around at the strange room. When she heard her friend Nalini's voice it all came back to her – the burning ghat, the sadhu and Kali.

"Nalini, how did I reach here? Where is Kali? And the sadhu? Oh God. How can I go home like this? What will I tell my husband? I feel awful, Nalini." She began to sob.

Her friend soothed her fears, handed over a potion – the magic brew – which she had to feed her husband deceptively.

~~~~~~~~~~~~~~

Weeks tumbled into months and Jivi's hopes shed each month with her endometrium. She pestered Nalini, to contact Kali and the sadhu. Shipwrecked on this rock of insane desire she began to scare kids and their parents with unwarranted attention.

Her husband tried to console her one night. Deep concern etched his soft voice. "Look, Jivi. It is okay. I am with you. I don't mind being childless. You look like a piece of whittled stick! I know you have to deal with taunts and mean words. But what is the worst that can happen? You will not be included in certain ceremonies and a few women will ostracize you socially. Don't let that..." she burst into inconsolable tears. He retreated without completing his rehearsed speech.

"Nalini, I must meet swamiji again. Tell him I am ready to do whatever he says to be blessed with a child. *Anything.*Pleeeease?" she begged one day. Her craving had unsteadied her grip on judgment. Moved by her plight, Nalini contacted Kali.

More than a fortnight passed by in agony. Then Kali arrived.

"Listen, I met him yesterday. He was furious because he believes it is your fault that it didn't work," she whispered, stunned by the spectre before her. Hope flickered anew in Jivi's misting eyes as she hugged the cheaply perfumed Kali.

"What else did he say? What should I do? How much will it cost me? Do I have to meet him again? When do...."

"Hold it! I have come with detailed instructions. First give me a cup of tea." Kali wandered around the house her face a grid of greed and guile. Going back to the kitchen she sat on a stool.

"Listen, this is the last time I am helping you. And so is swamiji. This failure is humiliating for him. Anyway, let's think ahead now. The next moonless night is still many days away. You have plenty of time to do the swami's bidding." She slurped the tea.

Kali continued conspiratorially, "The swami will perform a very special puja for you but for it to be successful he needs unquestioning co-operation."

"Oh, anything, everything! Whatever he demands."

Kali's eyes were slits as she measured up Jivi. She felt assured Jivi's mania would take her beyond the bounds of ethics.

"Meet me at the same spot as last time. I will take this gold necklace you are wearing, as my fee," she drooled. "Because this puja is exceptional, it will cost you twenty thousand rupees. Cash. You have to bring triple the quantity of the paraphernalia you brought earlier. And come wearing black. It is very essential."

"Is that all?" Jivi was visibly relieved. She would have given a lot more.

"There is one more thing." Kali hesitated before speaking again.

"You will have to sacrifice an infant. It is your job to get one," Kali's whispered words detonated like a bomb.

Jivi plunged into a trance of horror.

"B..b..b…but where can I get one? And h…h…how can I d…d…do this?"

"Do you want your own child or no?" The voice was icy, calculative.

"I do, I do. Desperately! But…this way?"

Kali was irritated. She pulled out a piece of paper from her bag.

"Memorise this name and address then burn the paper. This person will do the needful for just rupees two thousand."

The paper trembled in Jivi's hand like it had ague. Kali eyed the necklace as she saw her dither. The interplay of her fixation and integrity created havoc in Jivi's already chaotic mind. Kali slunk out of the house, an expensive watch disappearing with her.

The vulnerability, the rapacity of a possessed mind! Kali's well aimed darts struck bull's eye!

On the appointed day Jivi accepted an innocent babe in exchange for a paltry sum. It was inert, drugged but she could feel its teeny heart beating against her bosom. She hastened into a shady lane. A cat startled her nearly clawing the bundle out of her clutch as she stifled a scream.

"Keep this baby," she heard a faint voice in her mind. It was hers. "But he will not accept it. He refused to adopt one, will he take in an imbecile's child?" she argued with herself. "He will never accept it. Nobody will. I will at least release it from a doomed existence."

Its mysterious logic enmeshed her mind in a convoluted complacency!

She heard footsteps behind her but each time she turned, stark murkiness yawned at her. Perhaps her wheezing conscience was trying to catch up with her. Wading back through dark alleys, she returned to the rickshaw she had hired.

"Quick. I have to reach in the next half-hour." Her voice was muffled through the pallu that covered her head and face. She dabbed her neck and chin with one end as she chewed on her dry lips hoping the driver had not seen her face.

Getting off at a designated spot, she paid him and staggered towards Kali lurking in the shadows.

"Move, fast! But first give me the necklace" she hissed.

Jivi grunted derisively through her anxiety. Fleetingly she wondered what had brought them together – fate, greed or fanaticism. She didn't care. The time to speculate on her actions was long gone. She handed over all the things needed for the puja as also the money for the sadhu.

As they entered the ominous burning ghat the potbellied frame of the swami loomed into view; Jivi's quickened steps echoed her thumping heart. She thrust the dormant baby in his hands to get its weight off her conscience. She completely deadened her mind to its feeble protest. There was no turning back she knew.

"Kali has the rest of what you wanted. Give them…" But Kali had disappeared. She looked around for her only to be blinded by sudden light.

"Police! Freeze!" ordered an authoritative voice.

Caught red-handed there was nothing she could say in her defense. The sadhu and she were taken into custody and the innocent baby, stolen from a nursing home, mercifully united with his devastated mother.

"How did this happen? Where did Kali disappear? Had she warned the police? And the baby? She lied to me, oh God, what was I about to do?" The questions cascaded with her tears but there were no answers, only penitence for her deeds as she languished in jail.

Her husband had testified that she had been paranoid but he couldn't believe she could go this far for a child. He wasn't even aware of her meetings with the sadhu, he affirmed.

Her friend Nalini was questioned too. She reiterated his statements giving a graphic account of how Jivi had come close to losing her mind in her inordinate desire. She asserted that she was unaware of Kali's dealings and knew nothing about the sadhu. She had met Kali through someone else and had simply brought the two together. That was her only involvement in the sordid affair.

The sadhu was awarded life imprisonment. Jivi finished her long, rigorous jail term and came out an old, wise woman. Kali had been traced; the necklace, twenty thousand rupees and the watch were recovered from her. After due formalities, these were returned to Jivi on her release.

Her husband let her keep them but didn't take her back into his life. He had been living with Nalini and they had a beautiful daughter.

Her elusive faith in 'tantra-mantra' (occult arts), the violent collision between her passion and reality had brought seismic shifts in Jivi's life; the simplicity and anonymity of village life gave her hope for finding contentment, self-sufficiency and integrity.

The Small Hours

By John Drudge (Canada)

He sat alone in his dimly lit study, the silence of the night punctuated only by the scratch of pen on paper. He was working on a new poem, one that had haunted his thoughts for weeks. The ink spilled words of dread onto the page, unbidden and unsettling, as though the poem itself had a life of its own.

The old clock in the corner ticked on relentlessly, its chimes marking the passage of time, but he barely noticed. He was consumed by the rhythmic swirling that seemed to seep from his pen and into the room.

The first whisper came as soft as rustling leaves or the pages of an old book turning in the wind. He looked up but saw nothing out of place. Shaking his head, he returned to his writing, his hand moving with an almost frantic urgency. The whispers grew louder, their words indistinguishable but their tone unmistakably mournful.

Then, the room grew colder. The poet shivered, his breath misting in the icy air. Shadows in the corners of his vision seemed to shift and writhe, coalescing into dark, indistinct shapes. He rubbed his eyes, convinced it was just fatigue, but the shapes remained, growing clearer, more defined.

As he stared at the shadows, they took form, spectral figures from the past - faces he had long forgotten. They hovered around him, their eyes hollow and their expressions twisted with a mix of sorrow and accusation.

A woman with ghostly sorrowful eyes, spoke in a voice that was both a whisper and a scream. "You took our lives; you took our words, and now we are bound to your torment."

The poet's heart raced. He tried to speak, to defend himself, but his voice was swallowed by the silence. Shadows closed in, their whispers turning to anguish.

Desperate, he grabbed his pen and scribbled furiously, trying to rewrite everything. But the ink bled across the page, forming words that twisted and writhed like living things. The more he wrote, the more the words seemed to pull at him, dragging him away from himself, and into a thick stilted darkness.

When he looked up again the figures were gone, but the room was now filled with a dense, suffocating haze. His hands trembled as he stared at the page before him, the words now hard as rolled stone and the ink solidified into black, oppressive matter.

Shadow of My Previous Birth

By TilKumari Sharma (Nepal)

Once when I was near stream of my village, there was evening time. The storm used to move hardly. The raining was there. The lightening was near. I used to look with fear. The day was of my birthday as in Dipawoli. I frightened and screamed with huge sound. Then there appeared a beautiful girl child supposed to be three years old. I thought the child was left here. The child used to play alone. I became wonderful that how beautiful this girl child was. I went near her thinking she was left herself because there was village near it. I attempted to speak with child. She looked at me deeply and lost immediately. I became puzzled and screamed again saying "mother and mother." The moon began to appear in the sky in her way and I ran away from there. I frightened.

I reached in my home after fifteen minutes. Seeing me, my mother asked me," Why are you quivering?" My sister asked me, "What happened to you?" I told them all incidents and losing of that wonderful girl child. My sister told me that the missing child was the previous birth of mine. I seemed nervous and asked about all.

My elder sister told me all about missing child. She told me about her birth and death. As she told me that the ghost child was four years older than me. Before four years of my birth, she was born. She was dead because of fever. Her birth date was in Dipawoli cow and Goddess Puja. She once used to keep polish ink or sign on her upper part of face. After that she was sick. When she was serious with fever, she died. Then people used to dig her tomb near stream and kept her there after her death. That was her incident.

After one year of her death, my mother used to give birth to another girl child in her birth date as in same day of Dipawoli Puja. The sign of her ink on forehead appeared later in another child. That wad I as she told me. She told me that I appeared in her form with same sign of ink in my forehead. So people used to tell me second birth of the former dead child. But I did not know consciously. Sometimes I feel that the people are digging my grave before my death. I feel hard to live with my honesty. What I tell people they understand with opposite way.

Once my older sister told me that she saw dream of me as goddess in temple as goddess of wealth and knowledge. From that time, she promised me never quarrel to me. This was amazing incident in my life. I knew nothing about rebirth. But I thought people blocked my everyway being near to give sympathy. I did not like them. Even my family never encouraged me in good deeds. My relatives used to make me lower. They could not see my progress. This was fact. I saw alive death and grave in my life that my family members supported my enemies' names. Perhaps it was rebirth to be huge artist/ author from grave. It was my real luck that I made myself winner but not winner from the blood of mine people, family members and few national friends. Another incident of my life was to visit the ghost of my younger brother. He was two years younger than me. He died early in his younger age. Once I used to go near the former stream which was near our field. He was in the grave of the field. When I reached in field at five o'clock evening, I saw small boy child who was going to the place of former girl child. I without fear saw that he was white in color and went to the place where former girl child used to play. I became nervous and looked regularly there. The storm was beginning. I stood and looked regularly. The boy child used to wait girl child. After one hour, the girl child used to be there. Both used to speak the language which I could not understood. They started to play. I looked and looked from another corner. The girl child used to be near the boy very much. She used to treat him as younger brother. She cared him much. She was amazing girl from the magical world. People did not believe about life after death. I too never in belief to ghost or life after death. I became puzzled and quested about mysterious birth of mine after seeing this incident. I see that there is another universe beyond it to fill life to dead bodies. The girl was in the dress of green leaves. It was wonderful that she used to be near me later. She was spirit of goddess. So she appeared.

I reached in the home and told about all things of two children and their meeting and caring to mother and sister. I see that there is another life beyond this. They also became wonderful. They talked about me and former girl. All similarities were there in same way. Another day at the same time, I took my sister and mother to see them in the same place. They could not be seen. They did not appear there. I became sad that they would thought me I would be liar in front of them. Next time when I was alone near stream at mid 12 O' clock, I saw these two images at the beach of stream. I looked deeply that they were same children which I saw earlier.

I became wonderful and thought that the scientists were not perfect in the world to find out every truth. I saw them with my naked eye that these two children within time to time. I decided to search them that they were my own blood in underground den as the earth had transformed their soul to another world. So I could only saw them. Then I did not fear to them and attempted to near them. They were my own blood and I loved them much thinking about mysterious world. I thought that they were transformed in another form. So they appeared only to me as being same human being. When I did go to very near, both disappeared immediately.

I wept to remember them and asked god to keep them in safe place. Once my elder sister told me, "You came in the form of former dead sister. So you were like her." She told me, "You were goddess of the earth to have humanity". Really I felt so. I felt often as dead in this society. I felt insecure here. I saw many graves to me before my birth. So I saw the one shadow of mine in her. I felt myself as goddess of truth in front of earthly liars. The greed and lust have kidnapped the women and men in this earth. What gave moral lesson by me that they might emblem me negatively. I was in the underground den to fight against enemies who saw me as **scam** or **unreal**. I used to fight with them. So her shadow had supported me from the core of earth. Then I believe in the earthly power or holy power.

My former birth was really painful that they kept me in hard torture. Then again I took birth from same womb as being winner myself. So my forehead had natural victory of the truth. The ghost like shadow used to make me aware of grave diggers. These two children made me conscious to risk of life and living. They taught me what the death after life. After death, there is only shadow to round. Nothing more valuable was in the torture of life. The shadow of my former birth appeared like robot in the scientific world. The science often used to fail to know the magic of the earth that my shadow of death becomes my hard journey of life. The soul of former child was in me to rise again from the fire in my birth.

She transformed soul to me and used to hover in the earth as undead child. Perhaps people graved her before her death or the harsh human kept her in tomb with her aliveness. So she might took birth in me as revolutionary sound to change the injustice of the earth. Perhaps she might come in my mother's womb again to kill evil germs of life. She might enter in my soul as being fighter to bring new revolution to woman dignity and virtue. So as being rational writer I became puzzled to see the missing picture of my lost elder sister who gave me much consciousness about dead people and their eternal silent conversation to me.

I thought that it was my former shadow. This shadow was hovering in the world to rise me from grave. Now I became undead entity in the earth. Words carved the sculpture of mine in my former grave. Missing child girl was my security being to keep me in safe and secured place. My former birth had taught me I am goddess to bring horror like flooding, volcano, lightening, storm, and earthquake and so on when I am deeply with heart pain. So I thought she would help me to live eternally. Ghost like girl child was my shining shadow to keep me alive. So I was born on Goddess Day.

The Open Coffin

By Sushant Thapa (Nepal)

Marvin walked away from the happenings in his village. Nobody knew where he went. The newspapers were silent about him. The place where he worked was a cemetery. He was the guard at the cemetery gate. He used to prepare the list of the dead, and bury them accordingly. The village of Prata was a busy village. People worked throughout the day at the market. They sold goods and there was a line of coffin makers in the bazaar. Marvin had heard that souls disappear and now he himself had gone out of touch. The name lists of the dead were increasing and he was nowhere to be found. If the cemetery would be closed, the dead would have no abode to rest in peace. This worried the villagers.

The gateway to any life is the soul. It is also what needs the cleansing. Marvin had left behind him a note, in his room. It was written on it "Is Life a gift? I want to ask death."

The villagers gathered under a large Banyan tree. It was the afternoon hour and the clock was striking thirteen. The relatives of the dead people did not contact any coffin makers because they moved to the next village to bury the dead. That was how the dead did the business with the living in the village of Prata. That was all happening in the ghostly afternoons. This information circulated in the ghostly afternoons.

People were somehow scary of the night because the night was a mystery without Marvin.

In the discussion it occurred to the village head that the former dead should be dug out and the newly dead should be buried in their place—this was the weirdest idea that came out of the village head. The village head thought that he someone saved the space for the dead. Marvin had a friend called Dido and Dido did not like the idea. The village head assigned Dido to contact Marvin, but Dido was unsuccessful except finding that note in Marvin's house.

Marvin let out an extreme shriek of laughter when his guru told him that dead can be brought to life. Marvin thought there was no need of his job at the cemetery if dead can be brought to life. Everybody would be alive anytime. Marvin was all set to find the answer to this quest—he somehow had already understood by this time that death was necessary.

Marvin and his crow traveled together. The crow would sit on his shoulder. Marvin was seeking to talk with death. Marvin had always thought that death would be a person—but it turned out that death was a philosophy. Marvin heard the philosophy of death by the holy people. He set out to meet every ascetic—he met a few of them on his way to the cave. Marvin felt a deep quest to know where the dead went—and for that he got his answers from the living ones. It took time for Marvin to understand that death was unavoidable and it was as holy as life. Some poets told him that when the circle of life meets, one reaches the state of celebratory and accepted death.

So, Marvin was learning and he took some time out of his life to understand death and its philosophy.

Marvin met the Aghoris who kept the skull of a person and considered it holy. Marvin spent some time with them, and he learned about Maya, Moha and Mokshya.

So, Marvin decided to return back to his village. He decided to quit burying dead ones at the cemetery. The village head again interrupted. He did not like the idea of Marvin to quit burying the dead. Marvin and his crow had seen a lot outside of the village—they saw a Sadhu worshiping the dead skull—death was called Mokshya. Marvin felt like he was resurrected from the dead. He felt like he got his life back—but from the dead. Marvin would sit beside the cremation fire and he would see the priests performing the act of chanting mantras and honoring the dead ancestors. Marvin felt death was holy and we should do our Karma. The dharma of death was its Mokshya. Marvin grabbed the concept because his background as a cemetery gatekeeper helped him to satisfy his thirst for meaning in death.

The ritual of honoring the dead ancestors was prevalent in the Hindus. They did *Shraddha* every year in the name of their dead ancestors. Marvin saw the priest doing a puja for remembering the dead. It was all pious—to die was to be remembered.

Marvin went to the coffin shop in the bazaar and he called the owner. Marvin asked him to leave making coffins, and honor death. Death meant freedom for Marvin and he considered it be pious from now. The village head liked Marvin's idea of not making the coffin, but that would result in rotten dead bodies all over the village because the dead would not be buried or burnt. Marvin was called to the house of the village head.

"How do you plan to handle the dead ones?" the village head inquired.

Marvin was speechless; he had no idea.

He started thinking and he said, "I will find this answer too."

Marvin thought to ask the dead how they would like to be treated.

But this was a deep contemplative state in which Marvin was deeply drenched. Marvin was deeply moved so he went to the village of Mokshya to meet their village head. The village head of the village of Mokshya was a religious man. He was the priest of the dead. He felt that Marvin honored death, so he suggested that Marvin continue his job. The village head of the village of Mokshya and Prata talked with each other. They finalized that the dead should be honored and people die fighting for a good cause too, and that every day many young and innocent people die.

After hearing the talks of these village heads, Marvin felt that those who develop nuclear weapons should not do so, and no one has the right to take away the life. Life is an open coffin. The dead should not be thought that they have lost something unique. The world is an open laboratory and people need to reflect the deeds of the dead when they were alive. Their contributions needed to be analyzed—that way the dead never die and the coffin of death will forever remain open.

Marvin thought fiction lives on, the world lives on and memories keep following us. He read the paradox of life in the poem of William Wordsworth which said: "Child is the father of man." The man never dies in his life, he keeps on remembering his childhood and the childhood never dies in the whole circle of life. The closed coffin teaches us that life is an open coffin. Such is the fate of death that makes us want to contribute from our side, we keep on living in history, culture and study about life and death.

In Nepalese stories death comes as a Sepoy from heaven and gets locked inside a tree by a boy—people stop dying and the world gets over populated. Marvin studied that story and comes to know how the god himself had to descend down to free the Sepoy. Marvin's version of life was about understanding death. Different myths and legends regarding death appeared before him—that gave him shivers down his spines.

One night Marvin was listening to the song Fear of the Dark by Iron Maiden. He felt shivers in the dark. He was walking near the cemetery. The gate was closed and the moon seemed to be howling in the dark. The wolves were howling at unseen distances too. As soon as Marvin opened the gate of the cemetery which had been locked for many months, the bats flew out in large groups from the open gate and Marvin really felt that life was an open coffin. He continued his job at the cemetery.

The Graveyard shift

By Shiva Neupane, (Nepali-American Writer)

Rakesh Jetted off to Australia on 20 April 2007. After few weeks, he joined security job as a night patrol guard in Melbourne. He was given an induction by his team leader Prakash on his first night about how patrolling needed to be done at the cemeteries. The shift started from 10 pm to 6 am in the morning. On the first night Rakesh did patrol with Prakash in the various cemeteries in and around Melbourne. On his first night, Rakesh Seemed confident in how they patrolled around the various cemeteries every two hours or so. When it came to reporting incident, Rakesh wasn't too sure about how to report them and hand over to the security control room. The incident reporting task was done by Prakash on the first night and Rakesh had to learn on his feet how to submit incident reports and photos of the graveyard every two hours or so because on the following night Rakesh had to patrol the graveyards on his own.

He finished his first shift in the morning after patrolling whole night in and around the cemeteries. The day was very hot, so upon reaching his apartment in Epping, he put the air conditioner on and had a siesta for a few hours. He woke up in the evening and got ready for night duty. He stocked a few energy drinks in his car to sip on during the night for keeping himself awake.

As soon as he drove past the intersection light at Craigieburn road in Wollert, the torrential rains and thunderstorm distracted him from driving and he had to pull his vehicle into the emergency lane. The road was blanketed with hailstones and twigs of trees on either side of the highway. After a while, when the rain came to a grinding halt, he started his car and drove all the way to the cemetery in Bendigo. When he reached the site, the rain fell again, and a thunderstorm took place. He remained inside his car. The emitted light from the thunderstorm flashed over the Epitaph momentarily. And the trees' branches fell over the cemetery and hung higgledy-piggledy.

The dance of flickering light from the tapered round light on the pole scared him off while it flashed over the cemetery decors. The light from the pole and the reflective light from the cemetery décor, along with the flocking of kangaroos in the graveyard, caused a bizarre tapestry of fears that sewed itself into his mind. He falsely perceived ghosts owing to the movements of kangaroos and got trapped into surrealistic world that existed in his mind—thanks to the occurrence of pareidolia. After some times, he wanted to get out of his car to use portable restroom.

However, he could not get out of his car because of the mounting psychological anxiety and fear in his mind. He suddenly became unconscious in his car, his car seat was wet, he was sweating and radio's battery was flattening. There was no line of communication between him and the control room. The control room officer sent Samir the duty manager, to the site. He saw that car was aligned with the fence of graveyard and the guard inside the car was unconscious and laying his chest flat against the handle, with both hands dropped towards the brake, and he looked as though he was dead.

Samir took the first Aid kits out of his first aid box, opened the car door, and asked Rakesh, 'Are You Okay, mate?' When he didn't get a response, he checked Rakesh's nose and put his hand on his chest. He found Rakesh breathing. Samir applied some ice packs to Rakesh's neck and face. After a few minutes, Samir called an ambulance to take Rakesh to the hospital in Bendigo. The Paramedics took Rakesh to the triage for the admission and then to the emergency cubicle for treatment. According to his past medical history, Rakesh was diagnosed with anxiety disorder, and the fear and stress triggered by what he saw in the graveyard. The psychiatrist and doctor advised Rakesh to stay in the psyche ward for medical treatment for a few weeks.

He agreed and was moved to psyche ward. While the nursing station manager arranged a security patient guard for Rakesh, then he went berserk. His moods swung and became restless, aggressive, and confronted the security guard. This made health workers jittery about what might happen when it came to medicating him. The workplace safety issue was imperative for the safety of health workers and then patient himself.

A meeting was conducted regarding the patient's situation, and he received a mental health tribunal review for keeping him in the seclusion room for a few days. A patient watch guard was designated for him, who would monitor his pattern of behaviors from the door, which was left ajar. Rakesh kept getting irked at security guard because seeing the guard reminded him of being in the cemetery. The security guard was not a problem per se, but he became the medium through which he echoed all his anxieties and stresses from the cemetery. When there was no sign of letting up on his level of aggression, the health workers reviewed his job history and found he was doing a security job. This may have triggered him and escalated the situation in the seclusion room. The health workers advised patient watch guard to remain vigilant but keep a distance from him.

When security guard remained far from the patient, he became more relaxed and heaved a sigh of relief. This way, he was slowly cured by medicines and all the required mental and psychological therapies. When he acted as a normal person he was discharged from the hospital and stayed at home under medication. However, after a few days, he refrained from taking the prescribed medicine, thinking that he was fit in social environment.

One day, he was heading to the Great Ocean Road with his housemates for a day trip, upon seeing the cemeteries on the road side he got reminiscent of the past incident, the sky was murkier, the thunderstorm was striking the clouds just above the cemetery and the road was blurrily treacherous, he got distracted which inflicted a panic attack in him and he lost control of his car and subsequently he went off the road and somersaulted multiple times, and the car eventually stuck in the bush.

Rakesh sustained serious chest bruising and lacerations to his head and neck from the shattered windshields. He was unconscious in the lush green bush the wind was murmuring through the shattered windshields. The two glowing headlights in the lush bush caught Adam's attention, who was driving a taxi. He pulled over into the emergency lane and immediately switched on his hazard lights so as to alert other incoming vehicles on the highway to take road safety measures.

Adam got out of his car and walked over the gradient towards Rakesh's car. He tried to open the front door on a driver side but he couldn't do so owing to the door being jammed. The twigs, foliage and branches of a tree were stuffed into the car; Adam slowly took them out bit by bit and made some room to open the door. As he shone the light from his mobile phone by opening the door, he saw Rakesh lying on the seat unconscious, with tributaries of bloods from his head, neck and forehead running down his body and soaking the seat completely. Adam saw two boys in the back seats; the one sitting on the left side was Hari, who had laceration on his skull, and the one setting on the right seat was Deepak, who had lost his incisors and some premolars.

Adam started shivering upon seeing the tragic incident. He tried to call triple zero to seek medical attention for Rakesh and the two boys, but he dropped his mobile phone quiet often as he shivered while dialing the number. After making few attempts for calling the ambulance, the paramedics came to theirs' aid and took them to the Apollo Bay Medical Centre. Unfortunately, Rakesh died on the way to hospital due to the excessive bleeding and bruising on his chest. However, Deepak and Hari survived after administering medicine for a week. The dead body of Rakesh was kept in the mortuary room at the hospital for the relatives to pick up.

Since Rakesh did not have any relatives in Melbourne, his friends Deepak and Hari collected money from a go-fund and dispatched his body to Nepal. The Van picked the dead body from the Tribhuvan International Airport at Kathmandu and took the dead body to the Pashupati Arya Ghat for cremation. The family members became horrified while seeing Rakesh's face being uncovered as he was taken out of casket and placed on the pyre.

The mother, Radhika couldn't bear the agony and collapsed on the ground as Rakesh was their only one son in the family. The father, Rameshwor tried to console her saying that if something had to happen, it would happen. The Murphy's Law cannot be altered. Our son went to Australia to pursue a Utopian Life there but met with a Dystopian Life instead. Rameshwor hugged his wife, Radhika, as she couldn't afford to roll back her tears at seeing the dance of hungry flames over the dead body of their son.

Battle of Powerful witch's Family

By The Anonymous Hand (Phillipines)

Just keep me under the name 'The_Anonymous_Hand'; grew up, thought, and graduated from school in a small town, located in southern Philippines. The story I will share with you is based on the author's true to life experience when I was still studying. I was twenty years old at that time.

Ever since I was growing up, I have longed for having a physician, albularyo or what is called a 'faith healer' in our family. On my father's side. I don't know if it's just a result of the tradition from our ancestors that has been passed down from generation to generation in the family I grew up in.

Or, it could be just a result of being like other Filipinos who have amulets or charms on their bodies. Because someone like me has many questions about the mystery of this world. One of them is that I have a curiosity to discover many things that are in my mind.

And in my explorations, I always see and observe my uncle album's, whom I will keep under the name 'Uncle Delfin'. I saw his talent. I saw his skill. I saw how he treated his patients.

I saw his simple method of treatment, such as applying hilot-hilot to the lame using banana leaves with virgin coconut oil. Applying strange leaves that can heal the body of the sick. And that is accompanied by strange whispers that I cannot understand.

It is as if he is releasing a strange prayer or oration from his clenched fist. Then he will blow it on the injured patient. Presto, his patient will be healed. Isn't he great?

Because one of the things I learned is that those like them. My uncle was blessed by heaven to be a warrior of goodness. And I also believe that those like him will inherit glory in heaven.

****

"IS WITCHCRAFT really real? How do they do the spell? What happens to the person they are bewitching?" I innocently asked myself.

At that time, I was currently on the roof top of our house to feel the cold wind caused by the approaching Christmas season on my body.

I sighed one after another. Then I took the notebook that was inside the bag that I was carrying when I went to the roof top.

I opened a few pages of the notebook to look at some pictures. I was amazed by the pictures I saw. Pictures about ancient times while a woman wearing black clothes was using black power. And in the picture I was holding, I could see a black candle placed on a skull.

I closed the notebook and put it back in my bag and just lay down with my hands clasped together. I'm going to try to take a nap because I'm sleepy at that time.

I haven't slept much yet. When suddenly I was awakened. I heard someone calling in front of our house.

And what I didn't expect, those questions I had to myself would come true. A fulfillment that I would witness with my own eyes what the spell really was.

****

WHILE I was on the roof top of our house and continued to ponder the questions in my mind. I heard a man's voice calling my Dad. He called my Dad's name repeatedly and loudly. I got up and peeked through the gutter of the roof because the man's voice was familiar to me.

I wasn't wrong in my assumption. One of my uncles was in front of our house. My Dad's youngest brother. I frowned when I noticed that my Dad's youngest brother's face seemed to be restless and his face looked restless based on his body movements. Out of curiosity, I went down from the roof top to be curious about what they were talking about.

My Dad let his brother into the house. After sitting on the sofa, my Dad immediately turned to his younger brother and asked why he was so restless in the morning. And I heard Dad's questions as I was coming down the stairs to the living room to his youngest brother about what had happened!

Dad's brother told him what he had done to him. I saw his brother handing Dad a letter, which I heard was from their cousin in the town of San Juan. I immediately noticed Dad's frown when he saw the letter on the yellow paper. When he held the letter in his hand, he immediately handed it to me to read the contents.

I didn't hesitate. I immediately read the contents of the letter in front of them. I read the letter out loud. What the letter I was holding said was that they had to go to San Juan? My grandfather's younger sister was seriously ill. Grandma Maria. I didn't read anything in my letter about what that illness was.

After I read the contents of the letter. My father immediately ordered his youngest brother. He told him to go immediately to uncle Delfin and that he might leave suddenly. And he should follow their father to his house.

My youngest uncle immediately agreed to my father's order. He also said that he would tell his wife to pack clothes to bring. After that conversation, he said goodbye to his father and quickly went to his house. To tell his wife. And then hurriedly went to the albularyo brother and my Grandfather.

****

AT THAT TIME it was just the two of us in the living room. Out of nowhere, I was asked if I would go to San Juan with him.

I didn't flake at all. I told my father that I would go with them and wouldn't leave them at home. Because I also want to get to another place and I don't have anything to do either.

My father nodded. He told me to help my mother pack her things and said that he would quickly go to her cattle and buffalo before we went to San Juan.

And a few minutes later, I saw my father take his bolo from the pole he hung on the house and put it on his waist and quickly leave the house towards the hill to check on the tied cattle and buffalo that were our livestock that were used to earn a living.

I was filled with joy as I helped Mother pack the things to take. I feel in myself that my destination is a happy journey, I am sure of it. Because of the pleasure I felt, I did not eat properly.

TWO HOURS LATER! The people who will be going to San Juan are already in front of our house. My grandfather, my father's youngest brother and his wife. Of course, my father and mother are with me. And of course, our trip will not be complete if we do not have my uncle, the faith healer, with us. He is carrying a small bag that I think is his medical supplies.

Mind you, there are seven of us going there. My younger sisters will be left at home for the time being because there will be too many of them if they come along.

The things my companions were carrying were remarkable. They brought a lot of things with them that I think they might take San Juan for a long time because they don't know what Grandma Maria's condition is. What is this disease?

Grandfather immediately asked us that when everything is ready we have to leave. It is said that it is difficult and that we may even have dinner on the way there.

We didn't speak yet, they each carried their own bags. I immediately took the bag containing our things. And then we all went to the road to wait for a jeepney going to town of Rosario.

It wasn't long before a car passed by that was going to the town of Rosario. We immediately boarded and after a while, we were all on our way. While the car we were riding in was running. It's like playing in my mind what my Grandma Maria could look like when she's sick. It says in the letter that he has a serious illness, but the person who sent the letter did not mention what kind of illness landed on his body.

*****

Our group's journey was FAST! There were not many obstacles on the way because the Christmas season was approaching. What I mean is, there were no beings that could stop us from making our journey! We had a faith healer with us who could be prevented by evil elements from reaching our destination.

But I know for myself that no evil elements can stop us, because as soon as we boarded the passenger vehicle, uncle Delfin let out some Latin words into the air. I can see it clearly because I am always observant of my surroundings and all his movements and actions, I see. But there is one thing I don't know. What did he say to the air? I am convinced that only my uncle, the faith healer, knows that.

****

Five hours later, we reached the town of San Juan. Dad and Grandpa immediately looked for a ride. After a while, two tricycles parked in front of us. Those two tricycles would take us to the remote barrio where we were going. To Grandma Maria's house. I don't know who the driver of the tricycle we were riding was? All I noticed was that Dad and Grandpa were happily joking with them.

I sat in the back of the vehicle. Nothing, I just wanted to sit there. Because the cool air touching my skin felt good. Add to that the green surroundings we were passing through.

I admire what I see because it is so green on both sides of the road. If you look to the right, you will see the dancing rice fields that seem to be sprinkled with gold that can be harvested any day. While on the left side, various vegetables such as pumpkin and eggplant can be seen. There is no trace of anything happening in that place that is scary. For me, it is a paradise.

After a few hours of traveling, we finally arrived at the place we were going to.

The several hours of travel are over. My journey is over, my eyes filled with beautiful scenery as we make our way to Grandma Maria's house.

When we arrived there, a man in his thirties greeted us. He looked happy to see us. It turned out that he was our cousin and that he was Grandma's son if he was bedridden. Never mind that he was Grandma's nephew. He happily greeted us and welcomed us into his little home.

The whole environment was peaceful and airy, the breeze was cool and fresh, as the Christmas season was approaching. The crops were turning green because the soil seemed very healthy and was really good for growing various types of vegetables. The whole environment was peaceful and airy, the breeze was cool and fresh, as the Christmas season was approaching. The crops were turning green because the soil seemed very healthy and was really good for growing various types of vegetables. A typical country house song. That was one of the things I noticed on the ground, so it was not surprising that the plants were growing healthily.

"Is Maria awake now? Can we talk to her?" I heard my Grandpa ask Grandma Maria's son.

"Oh, Uncle! Mother is sleeping now. You can visit later." This was his response, along with preventing Grandpa from visiting his younger sibling. So we all decided to take a walk in the vegetable gardens around the house.

****

AT NIGHT, everyone decided to go to where Grandma was lying before we ate dinner. My Grandpa entered the room first because he was the older brother and Uncle Delfin followed. I didn't let anyone hold me back, I went inside because I wanted to see what was happening firsthand.

Grandma was talking to her guests so affectionately that you could tell she wasn't feeling anything in her body. One of the things I noticed was Grandma Maria's fingers that seemed to be turning black, as if they had been put in hot water.

I couldn't help myself. I secretly shed tears because of what I had witnessed. Pity overwhelmed me. My grandfather, my father and mother, and my uncles couldn't help their own emotions when they saw Grandma.

"Aunt! What happened to you? Who is the crazy person who ruined you like this?" Uncle Delfin asked one question after another while standing next to him and kneeling. He held both hands with his fingernails as if they were about to fall off.

"I don't know, grandson… I don't get angry with anyone here and above all, I don't fight with anyone because you know I'm getting old." Grandma Maria said to uncle Delfin. "Brother... Please help me! I'm in such a difficult situation." She pleaded as if asking for help from her older brother.

"God has mercy, Maria. Don't worry, my son is with me. He will take care of you, we will get rid of that."

"Yes, Auntie! I will take care of you first. Just have faith in God and he will help you." Uncle Delfin comforted.

For the second time, I could not control my emotions. Pity and horror overwhelmed me. Grandma Maria was in such a difficult situation. I could see in her eyes the intense torture of the person who had cast the spell on her.

"Get a candle, clean water and a bowl and I will cast a spell so we can see and know who did this to Auntie!" He calmly ordered the people present.

Everyone who heard moved. After a while, uncle Delfin quickly prepared the necessary tools for the castration he would perform. In front of him was a white candle, a spoon, and a medium-sized bowl filled with water and a mug.

He took the white candle, closed his eyes, and then whispered into the candle he was holding. After muttering the word in Latin, he rubbed the muffled candle on various parts of his hands, feet, forehead, and finally his stomach. In my knowledge, the albularyo could see and feel the element that had boiled in his grandmother.

He asked for a lighter and lit the candle he was holding. After a while, the drops of candle in the water began to take shape. And they wondered what had come out of the alum? Because it was the figure of a black woman. A fierce witch. A strong and high-level knowledge from the secret wisdom of the devil.

"Shit, the witch is to strong. I'm not sure if my knowledge will succeed in his knowledge. But, I will do everything I know to win the spiritual battle." This is a confession to all of us who have witnessed what he is doing.

****

"WHO DARE YOU BE!" A voice came out of my grandmother's mouth. Grandma's eyes sparkled as she looked at my uncle. I was surprised, Dad and Mom were Dad's brother and his wife. Other people who were curious outside the house were also surprised because a different voice came out of her mouth.

"Be honest with me, old witch! What sin did this old woman commit to make you torture her like this?" Uncle Delfin calmly asked the witch, then poured water on Grandma Maria's hand. We, the audience, were amazed when we saw part of Grandma's hand smoke and it slightly writhe in pain. Her eyes widened even more as her hands tried to reach the albularyo whose hands were currently tied so that she couldn't struggle or hurt him.

"You dare, you albularyo!" Grandma Maria shouted loudly. Grandma Maria struggled hard, and because of the force she was using, the rope that was binding her hands and feet suddenly snapped.

In the speed of events, a hand pushed the albularyo's chest. With the force of the force that hit uncle Delfin, he leaned against the wall of the house.

"Son of— I almost did it, ah! The strength of that witchcraft animal. I can't do it alone!" complained my uncle albularyo while dragging his back because of the wall of the house.

The men inside the house immediately acted. Even though they were hesitant and worried about the strength that Grandma Maria showed. They had no choice. They took another rope. The thicker and stronger one. So that it could bind the entire body of my poor grandma.

They quickly grabbed Grandma Maria's hands and feet. They did that so that it could no longer attack the albularyo. From my observation of what was happening. I could not imagine that a person's spiritual strength could be that strong when possessed by a minion of darkness. Because at that time the witch was the one who controlled Grandma Maria's body and she was also the one who was fighting spiritually with Uncle Delfin.

After a while, ten men worked together to tie up Grandma Maria. My grandmother was so weak at that moment that she quickly fell asleep. I think the black witch also had a hard time fighting my uncle.

What surprised me was that Uncle Delfin couldn't kill the witch. Why? I asked myself.

Outside the house, I heard women crying. I even saw my mother crying loudly. Maybe it was because of the pity she felt for Grandma and anger at the person who did this to her.

It was really difficult to explain what was happening around me. How could two beings from different perspectives on life and different forces fight?

****

SUDDENLY, the events of the past came back to my memories! I couldn't help but feel a chill, how could I have seen with my own eyes how Grandma Maria was going crazy while being restrained by almost six men? With Grandma Maria's thin body, how could someone like her be able to resist six strong men? Where did she get her strength if her only basis was her thin body?

But, how can I explain what I saw; the strength of the six men was useless against my grandmother. They were just holding on like children who could easily shake them off. The strong rope they put on Grandma's hands and feet looked like a thread that was being pulled tight.

Now I have proven that Uncle Delfin's statements have a point. The black witch's spiritual power is extremely strong. If they don't stop their fight, someone might end up harming the people who are stopping Grandma. At that moment I felt like he admitted to us that the black witch's skills were higher than him.

My uncle turned his attention to my father and the other men present. He said that he needed someone to help him fight the black witch. He said that if possible; they will take an antingero and not an faith healer. He added that the blakc witch only broke the living words he threw at them.

Uncle Delfin was happy with what the man said. So he sent them on their way. And said that every moment is important! You can't slow down because life depends on this opportunity. The witch is more powerful compared to him. They need to hurry before everyone is late.

The person who presented did not waste any time to go to the said antingero who is an acquaintance of theirs. After a few reminders and things to do while traveling. Two motorbikes were prepared and they quickly left.

I saw my uncle's attention turn to grandma Maria who was currently resting. His thin chest was still heaving as if there was no sign that the two forces had fought with each other.

I saw the beads of my uncle's sweat while he was wiping with the white towel he took from the pocket of his shorts. Then he walked out of the room with a limp. I think my uncle is feeling the pain he got in his side as a result of the collision with the wood of the house wall.

"Uncle Delfin! This is the water that Mother gave me. Drink it." I said to my uncle while handing him a glass of water.

My uncle thanked me before taking the water that I was handing him. He immediately accepted the water I offered. And then he didn't hesitate and quickly gulped it down. He even sat on a small chair while holding his shaking knee.

I couldn't help but smile because my uncle was cursing as he said; "That witch girl really got stronger. You'd think I was thrown against the wall. Even my strength and spiritual power were just drained by her."

Despite the events of that night. People couldn't help laughing because of his strange speech. Even I secretly smiled.

From my point of view, my uncle only said that to hopefully relieve the tension of the people present.

After a while, I could see the other people present, talking about their lives. Because I had nothing to say to them. I just preferred to just be quiet in a corner.

It was almost dawn at that time so everyone decided to take a rest. My uncle the herbalist and the other elders who were watching were planning to rest too. I thought that maybe they would gather strength to hopefully prepare for the battle the next day. And of course I would rest too. Because I wanted to see what could happen tomorrow.

On a pallet under a mango tree was the place I chose as a place to rest. Apart from the cool touch of the air, it seems that it is better to sleep there.

The next day...

The sun was already rising in the east when my father arrived with the three men with him. And on their return, I saw that the male antingero who they said had a high level of spiritual power was with them.

I no longer wondered why my father and his three companions were strong, skilled, and efficient antingeros? I learned that he was just a child when he was given an amulet by a forest hermit. Based on what I can see in the intensity of the man. I can say that he was only in his mid-30's. He was about five feet and seven inches tall. Just average height for a typical Filipino. His skin was brown and his body was slender as if he had been exercising. And he was wearing a medallion the size of five pesos around his neck.

From what I saw in that antingero. I am already convinced myself that the man with my father has the ability. I also saw some of the tattoos on his arm, chest, and back when he changed clothes. In my opinion, those are living words that were deliberately carved to serve as armor for his whole body.

"Is that you, Nards?" That's what I clearly heard from my uncle's mouth. It turns out that my uncle knows the man who is the sorcerer. He is currently talking to the man while sipping hot coffee. I heard that my uncle said that he didn't know that the man he was talking to was the antingero man who was an acquaintance of the three men.

My uncle sighed loudly and apologized for interrupting what he was doing. But he also thanked me because my uncle really needed his presence. Because of this case, he couldn't fight alone. He even said that just last night he had a hard time while fighting the sorcerer and that his allies might have called him.

"That's you, Nards." That's what I clearly heard from my uncle's mouth. It turns out that my uncle knows the antingero man. And it is currently talking to the man while sipping boring coffee. And I heard that my uncle said that he did not know that the man he was talking to was the antingero man who was known to the three men. My uncle sighed and apologized for interrupting what he was doing. But I thanked him because my uncle really needed his presence. Because of this case, it will not be able to win the fight alone. He also said that just last night he had a hard time fighting the witch and his allies might have called him." I even heard my uncle's sigh at the newly arrived antingero. Fisted it's still a bomb for the newly arrived man.

"Are your abilities as a healer weakening, brother Delfin! You used to be able to handle cases like this!" The man is serious about my uncle.

"My power is strong, no doubt! But not my earthly body, Nards! I'm just scratching and messing around right now. It's been a long time since I've heard of a case like this," he replied to the antigero he was talking to and turned to the people present. My uncle introduced the man to the people there. It also tells us that it has great power. And they are sure that they will defeat the black witch.

My mother came to us all. First, my mother invites the two men to talk before us. He said breakfast was ready on the table.

Despite what was going on, we all shared a happy breakfast that morning. I can't call it fun even though people are laughing. Because my grandmother is constantly lying on the mat of illness.

AFTER breakfast, everyone decided to go to Grandma's room. My mother was currently feeding Grandma Maria with the help of Aunt Teresa, I was introduced as Grandma Maria's son.

Uncle Delfin entered first, followed by my his friend, the antingero. Several men also entered, including my father. Those men, led by my father, would serve as the ones holding Grandma's hands and feet. What my father and the men would do was to stop Grandma Maria? They are the ones who will stop Lola

Maria when she becomes hysterical like she did last night.

When everyone entered, I noticed that the antingero had taken four pieces of stone from inside his shorts. They were very white. Smooth and rounded circles that you can deduce are holen. And they sparkled like diamonds when the light hit them.

He handed the two stones to my uncle. while the two stones are held together by it.

Grandma Maria's appearance did not change. Her skin was pale, her fingers were black, and she was very thin because of the pain she was going through. Her hands and feet remained tied to the bed she was lying on. Even though it hurt inside them to do that, it was because they had to do it. Because everyone thought that there was a possibility that it would break loose again and hurt again. They did not want to be afraid, that if they removed the rope that was binding grandma's hands and feet, the witch might be inside grandma's body.

Uncle Delfin and his antingero didn't take it any longer. After they perform the ritual of summoning and merging the presence of the black witch. We were all surprised when my grandma's eyes widened. That was proof that the witch was already inside her body.

Grandma's body immediately moved where the witch was. When it felt the presence of the albularyo and antingero, its eyes widened.

My uncle went to the grandmother's feet and the antingero took both of her hands. At the same time, they placed the stone on the grandmother's hand and foot. Then they squeezed together.

Suddenly, the grandmother screamed while the witch was inside her. "You're done with witchcraft!" I said to myself as I saw the grandmother's body writhe.

Her eyes were glaring, she was frantic and she was trying to reach out for the antingero. But he couldn't do that. She couldn't reach the antingero due to the intensity of the living words she let out. I saw the man raise his right hand and then whisper a finger. Soon, he lowered his hand and it went straight to the grandmother's neck, which you thought was being strangled.

She looked at us with a smile as if she was saying "One down!"

Later the antingero was suddenly stunned, how could it feel that another witch had entered inside the grandmother's body. It's male witch. Not just one, but a family felt that.

Uncle Delfin's friend Antingero told the people there that the witch was not alone, they were fighting an entire witch family. A witch family with a high level of knowledge from the secret wisdom from the devil.

My eyes widened, as did the people there. Now they understood why Grandma Maria was strong last night! That was the reason. Uncle Delfin was fighting a whole family of witch.

To be sure, uncle Delfin spoke to the witch who was in Grandma Maria's body. "Introduce yourself, witch! I want to know who you are and where you are from?" uncle Delfin asked calmly. The witch could not speak because of the intense pain he felt from being nailed to his body.

"I will repeat my questions to you, witch? Who ordered you to do this foolish thing?"

Uncle Delfin continued to talk to it. But it was stubborn. That's why the strong tools of the antingero and uncle Delfin were constantly applied to its body. They did it over and over again as if the two of them never got tired of what they were doing.

My grandmother continued to move, screaming in pain. The witch was very strong, very very strong. Because they were a family inside. I thought it might be anger from the death of one of her family.

While I was holding onto Grandma Maria's right leg, I could feel the strong force flowing through it. She was begging us to let her go but we were not listening to her pleas.

Later, I thought I saw a little light appear on the medallion on the chest of antingero wearing. I don't know if I just blinked or if the sunlight from the window hit it.

Due to the great strength of the witch family inside the grandmother's body, the ropes tied to her hands were broke apart into pieces.

Grandma Maria tried to get up quickly so that she could reach the antingero. The antingero moved quickly. He immediately took off the medallion he was wearing with one hand and quickly put it on the grandmother's neck.

Grandma Maria was crying while screaming because of the severe pain in his body. I heard from the antingero say that their all witchs souls would be burned and that they would not be able to survive the strong power of the medallion.

After several hours of spiritual combat between uncle Delfin and the antingero against the witch's family. The grandmother's body stopped shaking on its own. The heavy presence in that room also disappeared. That was a sign that uncle Delfin and the antingero had defeated the entire witch's family.

The entire family of witches died with the combined forces of uncle Delfin and the antingero. However, with the last breath of the chief witch. Blood came out of Grandma Maria's mouth, nose, and ears. That's why it happened, because they also killed Grandma Maria.

I sat down on the floor of the room weakly and bowed down while crying softly because of what happened.

I can consider myself that uncle Delfin and the antingero succeeded in killing an entire family of witches. But in return, Grandma Maria lost her life.

THE WHOLE FAMILY OF WITCHES IS NO LONGER, THE GRANDMOTHER IS ALSO NO LONGER.

****

Four days of mourning for the late Grandma Maria have passed. We have brought the deceased Grandma Maria, along with our other relatives, to her final destination.

While placing her in the tomb, I uttered a solemn prayer that God the Father would accept the soul of Grandma Maria.

As the day, month, and year progress. An event that I will never forget as long as I live. An event that I fully witnessed how uncle Delfin and his friend the antingero fought and ended the extermination of the entire family of witch, a highly educated witch from darkness.

And I always tell myself; I witnessed how the army of good fought against evil....

The Bending Bamboo in the Stream

By The Anonymous Hand (Philippines)

Just keep me under the name 'The Anonymous Hand'; grew up, thought, and graduated from school in a small town, located in southern Philippines. The story I will share with you is based on the author's true to life experience. At the time, he was still studying at the secondary school located in the next barangay. He was just sixteen years old at the time.

The author actually lives in a small barangay, which is full of mystery and wonders that surround it. The flying, blazing fire, or as others call it, the 'santilmo', are one of the example that he encounter. The games played by other elements with travelers bringing goods to Metro Manila.

And the scariest thing of all, don't forget that you have to honk your horn three times at the big trees next to the road you're going to pass; if you don't want the doll you're riding to swith off or have an accident.

Your author grew up in a simple, unpretentious family. In the word street language; a crow, a beak.

The author's father was a hardworking farmer, while his mother, when not working at home, sometimes accompanied him.

The author is the eldest of four younger sisters and the youngest is a boy.

Despite their simple, humble lifestyle, and limited financial resources, their parents managed to support their education. Their parents meet all their needs in daily life.

And now, your author is currently here in Saudi Arabia as an OFW.

****

YOUR author also had many wonderful experiences during his youth; which are still fresh in his memory to this day. They remain fresh in his memories and are not easy to forget; as if they happened to him just yesterday.

And one of them he will share is about the simultaneous bending of bamboo trees by the stream near the boundary of their barangay. The hairs on the back of his neck and arms cannot help but stand up in fear as each incident comes back to his memory.

In fact, as he wrote it, the author felt as if he were there and saw every detail of what happened with his own eyes, along with his three younger sisters. He couldn't help but ask himself; how did he manage to overcome the fear and terror that gripped his entire being?

This is how the author begins the story with the three younger sisters when they return home from work.

****

"OH, come on? It's getting late, Kuya. Our mother is probably worried about us," said my younger sister next to me. It was said to be his younger sister, because it was almost eight o'clock at that moment. And they still had a long way to go before they reached their home.

"What are you saying you're worried about? If you say so, he'll probably scold us!" the second is the one that follows it.

"Don't argue anymore. There's nothing else you can do. If we don't finish what we were tasked to do, what's the money we'll earn? It's also in addition to our school allowance," he reasoned with his two younger sisters.

He couldn't help but sigh as he held his two younger siblings back. When they didn't move, he motioned for them to continue walking.

A few moments later, as they continued their walk home, he could hear the three younger sisters laughing happily. He just remained silent while observing the surroundings.

By the way, the reason they were late at night was because he happened to be with his three younger siblings. They are siblings from a place where their job is to wrap chopped pork skin? Those wrapped chopped pork skin called 'sitsarongbaboy' are often found as an ingredient in lomi, gisado, and other restaurant dishes. While the rest is sold by the owner to customers at the market.

The money that we earn in two days of work is a great help to those like us who are financially poor? It's a big deal for people like us that we work two days to pay for school project, or other expenses so that we don't have to rely on my parent's.

As he continued walking with his three youngers siblings on the road. He didn't feel anything strange or afraid of the surroundings because his reason was; the moon was full. A big advantage for him to see the road. Which gives light all around. And because the moon is so round it seems like it also gives us light while walking.

After about one hour and thirty minutes of walking, they soon reached the place that was supposedly feared by all passersby. Especially the travelers carrying goods that were usually brought to Metro-Manila, and people who unexpectedly got caught in the dark while walking.

Many people say that this place is inhabited by kapres, malignos, and earthlings being. For me, it is not surprising, because the entire area seems mysterious because of the beautiful trees and plants planted here.

As they approached the area, he gently reminded his younger siblings to lower his voice, and they complied with his request.

After a while, the happy laughter was no longer heard from each other. All my siblings were seriously walking while clinging to me.

As they continued walking. For some inexplicable reason, the sky suddenly darkened. The round moon he had seen earlier suddenly hid behind thick clouds as if it didn't want to give them light on their path. Or, maybe he didn't want to see the strange creatures hiding in the darkness of the night.

"Take out the lamps we brought," he whispered to his younger siblings. "It's too dark for us to walk."

"Okay, Kuya!"

They quickly complied. They did take out the bottles with fill of kerosene and then he reached the lighter in his pocket and quickly lit them.

"Thank God. There is light now. Why did the moon suddenly disappear?" one of the younger sister complained.

His two other siblings breathed a sigh of relief because of the strong light coming from the bottle they were holding. That light is the one that gives light to what they walk on. The only surprising thing is, even though there is light on our way. It still stuck to him.

As they continued to walk, he couldn't avoid looking at both sides. He noticed the gigantic mango trees. Each of those leaves are lush and the plant is really beautiful and healthy as if someone is taking care of it. They were also tall, which was the same reason why the whole area was so dark.

When they reached the middle of the stream. Suddenly, an inexplicable phenomenon occurred. Suddenly, a wind blew throughout the area. The wind was only weak. It felt like a northerly wind. That we didn't feel that wind before. The wind was weak but why were the bamboos dancing around the road that surprised them so much. And other bamboos seem to kiss the tip on the road.

From what he witnessed, he couldn't explain what was happening? Suddenly he asked himself; is this the miracle that is happening in this place? If this is it, is it really scary? He couldn't help but feel the hairs on his back of the neck and arms stand up. As a growing youth. Fear enslaved him at that time and he didn't know what to do—whether to run or just stay where he was.

He wanted to run because of the fear he felt that was holding him back. He couldn't help but feel his head suddenly grow bigger. His body shook a lot because of the intense fear he felt. Being the oldest, he didn't reveal that to his three younger siblings. They tend to get scared and may lose consciousness. He knew that his younger siblings would be scared and he didn't want to be a burden to them going home looking like that.

Along with the wind blowing. The lamp her younger sister was carrying lost its light. When the lamp died, the path they were walking on became dark. They could no longer see the road because it was so dark. At that time, she felt as if a creature had deliberately blown us from above. Her other sister could not help but scream in fear. So they squeeze into my body.

Even though his knees kept shaking. He needs to get stronger. He thought to pray to God for help and for guide us.

For the sake of his younger siblings, he forced himself to be strong, having been overcome by fear and anxiety. He looked around, despite his fear, his forehead furrowed when he saw a small light flickering inside the bamboo. He was amazed, he didn't know why there was light coming from inside it?

"Sister's, pray the 'Our Father' while walking. That will help us gain strength and protection against evil spirits. Go ahead." he ordered his younger siblings.

"Kuya, I'm so scared..." his third sibling's hand trembled as he held onto his arm.

"Me too, Kuya."

"Kuya, don't leave us here."

"Fight the fear you feel. We too can get through this scary place. Just keep walking while praying to God and we will surely be heard. Go ahead," he ordered.

His younger's siblings followed him. They prayed together as they slowly walked, until he could barely see the road leading to them. Even though his chest was tight with nervousness, he continued walking through that dark and gloomy area.

After walking for almost a few minutes in that nightmarish place, they finally reached the point where they had completely passed.

Before he could understand the miracle that had occurred. The light wind that they had felt earlier suddenly stopped. The bamboo trees that had seemed to be dancing and their tips were still kissing the ground returned to normal.

The three younger sisters continued walking while praying. Until they finally passed and got away from that nightmarish place.

They were able to breathe a sigh of relief when they saw a Jeepney coming from their area. The driver of the Jeepney did not hesitate. He even honked his horn three times in the middle of the stream as a warning that they were about to pass.

When the driver met them. He immediately gave them a ride until they reached their home.

When they all arrived at their home. They were all sweating profusely because of the fear they had experienced that night.

"Mom, we were so scared at the stream." His voice trembled as he told his mother.

One of his younger siblings said the same thing. "Yes, Mom. We were really scared. It's a good thing that Brother didn't leave us…"

"Children, listen," their Mother told them, as if they had never experienced anything before. "What you experienced is the same thing your Father and I experienced? If you remember, it was only last month that we returned home early in the morning."

My mother continued to tell them stories while trying to calm the nerves they had experienced. She still remembered that day. There was only a slight rain. The moon was shining brightly in the sky. They were on their way home from town. Their father said that they had driven the car they were riding at full speed. But suddenly they were surprised, because when they reached the middle of the stream. The car's engine just stopped for some unknown reason.

Some passengers inside the car were very scared. The driver started the car's engine several times but the car still didn't want to start. Until one passenger suddenly shouted loudly.

"We'll apologize to you. We didn't do it on purpose. It won't happen again."

Suddenly, the car's engine started up. In fear, the driver drove the car slowly, thinking that the villagers living in that area would get angry again. They may have disturbed the residents of that area.

The driver continued to drive the car slowly until they finally passed that area and arrived at their respective homes.

Because of that incident, the news spread like wildfire in their barangay. That's why every car that passes that area—whether it's day or night, they don't forget to honk their horns three times and drive slowly as a way to let the earthlings residents there who they can't see go.

A MONTH later, his uncle, 'faith healer', visited. He didn't hesitate any longer, he suddenly opened the conversation to see if he knew anything about the strange phenomena happening in the stream at the boundary of their barangay.

His not hesitate answered my question. "Nephew, all I know is that the part of the bamboo grove in that area is believed to be a tunnel to the other world. 'To the world of fairy tales'."

He couldn't help but be amazed by what his uncle had revealed. At his young age, he had only just learned that such a world existed. He returned his attention and listened to his continued story.

"Regarding the beings that make themselves felt in that stream. They are guardians of the place. Those are earthlings, capres, and tikbalangs. I remember once when I passed by that place, it was also a full moon. I heard drums beating. I could hear them right inside the bamboo grove. But, don't be afraid because they don't hurt people. They just play with us." a long explanation to his uncle, 'faith healer'.

Over the days, months, and years, some other people still continue to avoid passing by that place at night. The reason for that may be because they have seen strange things happening in that place.

It was almost twenty-five years ago that he and his three younger sisters had their bad experience in that place. What they had experienced there was truly terrifying?

Now there are light poles in the stream, and the stream is no longer very pretty. The once dense bamboo groves and large branches are gone.

Once he passed by on the motorbike he had bought. As he traveled through the area, it seemed like the past was still coming back to his memories. The intense terror he experienced every time he remembered;

'THE BENDING BAMBOO IN THE STREAM'!!

The Cursed Radio

By RajendraOjha(Nepal)

In the distant mountains of Nepal, on a cliff that was hidden and clear with fog, was an old mansion that no one came to visit. Its cracked walls and shattered windows spoke volumes of suffering for the ages. It was that the mansion which was on eighty long wheeled broad mainly occupied two third floor many curves in back of its paras that it staffed somebody's radar turn down at. They said that no one came back the same from inside the rooms, so no one would go inside and rot in that uneasy silence.

It turned out that it was not the werewolf that Rajesh should fear. Soaring enclosure climbing led himself a broken family turned into unwanted loneliness. Three years passed without any Sita who went inside who disappeared under unusual circumstances, and despite every illusionary look for her he crossed, there had been no use. Life without love was intolerable, but such love had driven him mad. He had spent months lying down on his stomach on the floor studying numerous reproductions of old tomes on wizards, magic, ghosts and all other things where scientific knowledge lacked the courage to explore any further.

In one literally obscure antique shop in Kathmandu, Rajesh had found an old radio covered in unfamiliar engravings. There was a tattered paper with words: "For the impossibly stubborn." The owner of the shop, a wizened man with twinkling wisdom in his eyes, had lectured him against playing with it but Rajesh, willing to try anything for a piece of his beloved, paid no heed and bought the Radio.

The mansion was a place of haunting stillness, its long, empty halls echoing with the sound of Rajesh's footsteps as he carried the radio inside. Outside, the fog seemed to creep right into the walls, making them inhospitable as if the air itself was thick and heavy to breathe. Rajesh set the radio on a wood-framed table in the parlor, its dancing light from his candle sent extended shadows to twist grotesquely in many directions on the peeling wallpaper. The mansion was alive with a heartbeat all its own-the creaks and groans of the old house like labored breathing from some dying animal. The radio was antique, cold, and heavy, with unforgiving knobs against his skin. Rajesh's hands shook as he turned the dials, immediate static hissing into the room. Louder, almost unbearable, before suddenly ceasing. The oppressive silence that followed caught Rajesh for a moment, wondering if he had made a terrible mistake. But then, faint and distant, he heard a voice. "Rajesh?" The sound was weak, barely more than a whisper, but it was unmistakable: it was Sita.

Rajesh's heart was racing. "Sita? Is that really you?" his voice hoarse from disuse, but filled with a desperate hope. It was followed by a long pause, after which the voice replied, "Help me, Rajesh. I'm trapped... in the darkness between worlds.

Rajesh's breath caught in his throat. He had been afraid of this sort of thing, but he never had believed it possible. "Where are you?" he asked, shaking.

"In the echoes... in the spaces between words," Sita's voice answered him, fainter, it seemed with every syllable, as if she were being pulled away from him with every word.

Rajesh anxiously began to turn the dials again and again, trying to make the connection stronger. Occasionally, whispers of some supernatural being originated from the radio in a rough voice, and broke the silence of the hall. The night was yet to be passed, but for Rajesh this night was like a millennium. The radio aired Rajesh's obsession live all through the day and night. he spoke to it. But nothing fruitful was happening through this act. Days turned into weeks, and Rajesh's obsession with the radio grew, begging echo of Sita to say more, to help him understand how he might bring her back to the real world where she actually belongs to. But the more he tried to reach her, the more the house appeared to react-doors creaking open of their own accord, walls groaning as if something was pushing from the other side. Sometimes, he could have sworn he saw, out of the corner of an eye, fleeting shadows dart just beyond the edge of his vision, but when he turned, nothing was there. Soon, sleep became impossible. Every time he would shut his eyes, faint scratching sounds within the walls could be heard as if something was trying to claw its way out.

One night, with a storm outside, a new sound was produced by the radio—deeper and more sinister. From the static came a voice, and it spoke of malice that sent a chill down Rajesh's spine. "You shouldn't have interfered," the voice hissed wickedly.

Rajesh recoiled, his skin crawling with an inexplicable dread. "Who're you?" he demanded; his voice barely steady. It replied, "I am the guardian of the void. In that tone was mockery, ancient, as if empires had risen and fallen before it. You have disturbed the balance of the dead". The temperature in the room plummeted, and he could see his breath fog in front of him. The shadows fell on the walls and started to twist and writhe, as if alive, forming faces contorting silently with screams of agony. Rajesh felt an unseen presence lurking just beyond the edge of his perception; the cold hand brushed the nape of his neck.

He had hurled the radio against the wall, hoping to break it, but it resisted, still vibrating in shards with a life of its own. The malevolent voice grew louder, threatening. "Your love has bound you to this cursed place," it snarled-the words echoing off the walls, seeming to come from everywhere and nowhere at once.

During that very night, the radio started playing recordings of Rajesh and Sita's lives in a really spooky manner. It worked out the happiest moments to get haunting echoes of sorrow, while the mansion itself seemed to warp and shift. Halls extended and shrunk, placing Rajesh into a maze of memories and fear. The fabric of reality seemed to tear up around him, with Rajesh sliding further into madness.

The mirrors in the house began to reflect things not there: glimpses of Sita, her face twisted in torment, or flashes of dark figures lurking behind him. He began to hear Sita's voice calling from other rooms, turning to find them empty. Sleep-deprived and paranoid, Rajesh could no longer tell if he was awake or trapped in some nightmare from which he couldn't escape.

One night, the radio suddenly produced a deafening burst of static, and the voice that had become so malevolent shrieked out in a howling torrent, "Join us or be forever bound!

Rajesh entered a room he had never seen, shaking with fear. The walls were filled with dust and the air was thick with something rotten. A new radio, just like all the other ones, sat atop a pedestal in the middle of the room, untouched yet stirring in dark energy. He had just reached when the radio crackled into life, and Sita's voice came up-mechanical, from a distant: "Rajesh, destroy it before it is too late".

In desperation, he finally sought a means of release from his bad dream, Rajesh reached for a heavy book from the shelf and crushed the radio into pieces. Shrieks and wails are then filled within the mansion, walls starting to shake violently, rattling as if the very foundation was coming apart.

But then, in the same fractional moment, the din ceased. The room was silent again, and the threatening pall that had hung over the mansion since day one suddenly appeared to lift. Rajesh collapsed to the floor, worn out, feeling a deep, uncomfortable void in the places the fear had occupied.

Rajesh, breathing hard, espied a note lying on the floor next to the shattered remains of his radio. It was in shaky handwriting; the ink was smudged, as if with tears: "You were never meant to leave."

The note was signed "Kavi," a name he had never heard before from Rajesh. The confusion and chilling feeling sent him out of the room, wandering along the darkened halls of the mansion. Outside, the fog had thickened and pressed against the windows, heaving like some living entity and wrapping the house in cold dread.

Rajesh saw a ghostly figure standing in the fog at the edge of the cliff. It was Sita-or what was left of her. The translucent form danced like a dying candle. Her eyes, once a mirror of love and warmth, reflected back now a haunting medley of sorrow and relief, her mouth frozen in a silent scream.

Rajesh reached out to her, his heart breaking, but as he did so, she dissolved into the fog, leaving him alone on the edge of the cliff. The mansion fell into a deathly silence-a deathly silence that echoed into nothingness. But the silence was not reprieve; it was the silence of a predator lying in wait.

For a time, Rajesh lived in the mansion in comparative peace. The radio was destroyed, and the voices had gone silent. But the stillness of the mansion was only deceiving, for deep in its heart, something dark and ancient continued to ache, watched him, only waiting for the perfect moment to strike.

One evening, a package arrived at the door of the mansion, though Rajesh had long since stopped anticipating visitors. Inside the package lay another radio, like the first one, its surface without a single mark and polished to brilliance. Accompanying it was a note, in the same hand as before: "For those who continue to seek."

Time eventually made Rajesh get used to the radio, though he never dared to touch it. But with days passing, the whispers grew louder, more insistent-invasion into his mind, it seemed, even when he was far away from the room in which the radio sat. It was as if the mansion itself was trying to draw him back to it, to make him listen.

One night, the whispering reached a fever pitch and danced along the corridors, seemingly a thousand tortured souls shrieking in unison. Rajesh, unable to resist any longer, found his body moving of its own accord toward the radio. Outside, the fog had closed right in to where the panes were obscured completely; the world beyond the mansion lost in a sea of white. This suddenly ceased when Rajesh stood before the radio, followed by an intolerable moment of silence. His hand hovered over the dial, with a moment of hesitation, knowing full well that the repercussions of the twist in that dial were irrevocable. He finally turned the dial with his quivering fingers.

The radio crackled on, except this time it didn't produce any static, nor a mellow voice from ages gone by. Instead, footsteps emanated from the speaker: heavy, slow, and deliberate, as if someone or something was drawing near. Rajesh's heart slammed in his chest while the footsteps grew louder and closer until they were right behind him.

He spun around, but the room was empty. Yet the footsteps continued circling him, closing in. The air thickened with the scent of decay, and the walls of the mansion started to close in on him; the shadows stretched and twisted into horrific shapes. Then, the footsteps stopped, and Rajesh felt the cold breath upon the back of his neck. He didn't dare turn around, frozen into an all-consuming terror. The radio let out a low, guttural sound, like the growl of a feral beast, and the voice of the entity that had been haunting him finally spoke.

"You can never leave," it hissed, its voice a choir of a multitude of souls entombed in eternal torment. Rajesh screamed-a wild, desperate sound-but it was swallowed by the darkness that enveloped him. The last thing he saw was the radio dial spinning frantically on its own before everything went black.

When the villagers found it, weeks later, the mansion was as empty as it had always been, and silent. There was no sign of Rajesh-no indication that anyone had been in it. But the radio remained, resting on a shelf, untouched, pristine. Those who were brave enough to come nearer to the mansion from time to time heard, when the wind blew in their direction, footsteps from inside, accompanied by a soft, almost imperceptible whisper.

There was a new note beside the radio now, scrawled in that same trembling handwriting: "For those who cannot let go". And the house, leaning on the edge of the cliff, stood its vigil over this plain drowned in fog, as some forbidden place, into the depths of which the living is afraid to fall, lest they enlarge the innumerable line of those spirits that had been lost to the darkness.

The radio, at the core of the mansion, whispered on- just waiting for its next victim to tune in, merging them into one with the void, lost forever within an echo of what once was.

Belladona's Wrath

By Ythela Garcia (Philippines)

Angela gritted her teeth after the conversation with her elder sister, Alyssa. As her sister wept through the entire video call, Angela clenched her fist. She already knew the reason for her sister reaching out like that without even uttering a word. Angela had tried to talk Alyssa into breaking up with her philandering husband a bunch of times before, but the latter still chose to endure being a martyr wife.

Maybe there's some truth in the old saying that it is the daughter who pays for his father's sins. History tends to just repeat itself. But Angela promised to herself that she won't be like Alyssa, or Teresa, their mother.

AT A FAMOUS bar in Manila, Jude along with his friends are already planning to spend their week's wages on alcohol and women. He had no plans on coming home to his nagging wife. He had wanted to call it quits with her but he was sure that won't be possible with his family being on the conservative side. For them, marriage is sacred. But nothing can deny the fact that his love for Alyssa had long been gone. She couldn't bear him a child, and what's worst, she couldn't pleasure him in bed.

Jude bit his lip when a certain woman entered the bar. As she walked towards him, he immediately felt aroused. He couldn't stop himself from whistling as he gazed at her entire body.

She was wearing a black silk dress that at first glance would appear like just a simple nightgown, but it was enough to catch his full attention. It wasn't a fitted dress, but it clearly accentuated the woman's body, and her black stilettos added to her sensuous aura. Jude slowly lifted his eyes and was truly mesmerized by the beauty of the woman whom he didn't notice was already in front of him. He was no different from a high school kid that saw his ultimate crush. The woman had deep set eyes and pouty red lips, features that made Jude weak in his knees.

"Hi, can I join you for a bit? I'm just waiting for... a friend."

Jude was startled when the woman suddenly spoke.

"Anything for you, Miss...?"

"Belladona."

Jude was already used to those kinds of bar scenes and the games played by women who were partygoers like him and his friends. After exchanging some details about themselves, Jude shared drinks with Belladona. He wasn't sure if that was really her name but he couldn't care less. All that mattered to him at that very moment was spending the night with the beautiful, sexy, and seductive Belladona.

THEY GOT up to three rounds but Jude felt like it wasn't enough. She was different from all the other women he had met and made love to. It was only with Belladona that he felt true satisfaction despite her being a complete mystery to him. Jude wanted to ask for another round but shook his head as he noticed the woman was already asleep. He didn't know what compelled him to stare at the woman who was still so beautiful in her slumber.

His brows furrowed as he realized something about the woman's face. "Why didn't I notice this before? She looks so much like Alyssa. Maybe because now, her makeup's worn off because of sweat." He sighed after answering his own question. "Maybe I'm just too tired and drunk that I'm seeing and thinking of these things. Or is it because of guilt that I remember my wife all of a sudden?"

He dismissed the thought and lay on the bed beside Belladona. He wrapped his arm around her, with a tender smile on his lips.

ON THEIR way home, Gerry let his wife and their kids go ahead without him. He wanted to go to his male friend first, who was a godfather to his second daughter, Angela. However, when Gerry passed by the basketball court, Girlie startled him as she walked up to him. The woman put her arms around his neck like a snake. She was supposed to be a godmother to their youngest, Andrei, who had just been baptized that day.

Gerry knew very well that the woman was liberated, having lived in the city, but he couldn't just ignore what other people would think if they saw them. Gerry quickly handed her the money she asked to borrow, and then he left.

Meanwhile, at the baptism party at their house, Teresa wondered why her daughter Angela kept on staring at Girlie. Seconds later, the young girl approached her and pointed to the woman who was cheerfully chatting with Gerry among the other guests.

"That's her, Nay! The woman who was flirting with Tatay a while ago. They thought they were alone. They didn't know I was there hiding behind a tree. They're bad people, Nanay. Especially that woman, Girlie!"

Teresa was stunned with what her daughter told her. The girl was already crying by then but was still glaring at Girlie. Teresa asked Angela what else she saw, but the young girl only answered with sobs. Teresa thought her daughter just had a wrong assumption about Gerry and Girlie's closeness. Teresa called for Alyssa, her eldest daughter, to accompany Angela inside their house.

A week after Andrei's baptism, Gerry returned to the city for work. Girlie was supposed to travel with him but encountered some problems so she stayed at the province.

When the baptism pictures arrived, Teresa's family were beyond happy. Everyone was, except for Angela whose eyes were full of hatred as she looked at the picture of Girlie, there with a wide smile, latching onto their father's arm. Since then, Angela wouldn't talk to anyone. Teresa would only catch Angela talking to herself, which she figured was only normal for a six-year-old. That her daughter was just memorizing some poem or song for her class.

But one day, when Bernie, Teresa's godbrother, came for a visit, something unexpected happened. Angela caught sight of Bernie holding her mother's arm and in an instant, she had a sinister expression on her face. Teresa was shocked when the young girl pulled the knife from the thatched walls and pointed it to Bernie.

"Why are you touching my mother? Just 'cause my father's not here? I'll tell my Tatay! You're a bad person, too!" the young girl screamed, eyes flaming with anger.

As Angela was about to stab Bernie with no hesitation, Teresa yelled her name. Like cold water being poured on her, it stopped her rage, but for only a few seconds. Teresa reached for Angela but the young girl ran outside the house with the knife still in her hands.

"Your child almost killed me, Teresa!" Bernie finally said in disbelief. Embarrassed, Teresa apologized to Bernie and asked him to leave.

BEHIND the trees and crops, Angela cried out in anger as she repeatedly stabbed the ground with the knife. Her heart was consumed by hatred for those people who wanted to destroy her happy family.

When her anger subsided, Angela decided to return to their house. But as she walked beside the cornfield, she found her dog Angel and her pet cats all lined up on the ground, lifeless, their mouths foaming and eyes open. Angela felt her heart was crumpled as she couldn't believe what her innocent pets had suffered. Someone deliberately put poison around the cornfield to lure and kill them. Trembling, she fell to her knees, and swore to seek revenge.

THE NOISY ringtone of her phone brought Angela's conscious mind back to the present. She quickly answered the call when she saw it was Alyssa.

"Gel, my husband, Jude! He's dead! My husband is dead, Angela!" As Alyssa became hysterical, Angela was lost for words. Despite her hatred for her brother-in-law, she couldn't help but be overcome by grief.

"Please, calm down. I'm gonna wait for Andrei and we're coming over. Pull yourself together, okay?"

Angela hastily packed only necessary stuff, and she made sure that it'll be enough for a one-week stay at her sister's house. She texted Andrei and instructed him to go straight to her house, in the meantime, leaving out details about Jude on purpose.

Upon entering her room, Angela took a step back, and her eyes widened with shock. There in front of her was the person she never wanted to see, grinning and staring at her.

"B-Belladona..." she stuttered.

"The one and only. I figured you miss me and you need me, my dearest Angela, that's why I'm here again. Oh, by the way, I brought something for you, even though you look really surprised to see me. Now that makes me kinda upset. But I'm sure you'll love my gift."

Before Angela had the chance to ask what it was, Belladona quickly walked towards the box on her bed and excitedly picked it up. Angela froze as she saw what's inside. A revolting stench spread across the room, making Angela throw up.

"Aren't you gonna ask whose manhood and heart are these, Angela? They're your beloved brother-in-law's. Oops, hated should be the perfect word." Belladona let out an intimidating laugh. "I don't want to see you sad, hurt, or crying because of anger, my dearest Angela. That's why I found a way to get rid of your problem, and at the same time, your sister won't suffer anymore."

JUDE SLOWLY opened his eyes and found himself with his arms and legs tied up to the bed. Terrified, he screamed and tried to escape, but he suddenly stopped when he saw Belladona come out of the bathroom with no clothes on. Jude gulped and felt his manhood being aroused again, despite having finished rounds with the woman. His fear turned into lust as he wondered what Belladona was going to do. He thought she was really adventurous in bed, all the more reason for him to go crazy over her. In a flash, Belladona was already on top of him and Jude once again tasted the extraordinary pleasure and happiness only she can bring.

After making him satisfied for the fifth time, her eyes suddenly hardened as she looked at him. This change baffled Jude and distracted him from the excruciating pain of Belladona slashing off his member with a kitchen knife. Jude screamed in horror as the woman casually held that severed part of his body and showed it to his face, blood dripping on the sheets.

It all happened in a blink of an eye. Belladona went on top of him again as Jude desperately tried to escape. The woman stabbed him on the chest continuously while laughing like a maniac.

She only stopped when her arms grew tired. Before leaving the room, she dug her hand inside his chest and took out his heart. She put the heart and his other organ in a big plastic bag. She then placed the plastic bag inside a hospital bag.

ANGELA found it difficult to breathe.

"Y-You're the one who killed Jude?! Why did you do that? You should've just let karma take care of him, Belladona!"

Belladona pretended to be surprised at what she said, but before long, the woman laughed as if to mock her.

"Coming from you, Angela? So that's the reason you let karma punish Girlie, Bernie, and your grandpa Berting? Because you despise promiscuous women like Girlie, that you let her be bitten by a snake. Which she deserves, by the way, because she almost stole your father from your mother. Then Bernie wanted to steal your mother from your father, and almost raped her.

When he got too drunk and fell asleep by the cornfield, you stabbed him multiple times on his chest. And lastly, Lolo Berting, your grandfather's brother. You killed him, too, by putting poison in his food, just like what he did to your beloved pets. We're both murderers, Angela."

Angela took a step back, squinting her eyes as she felt a sharp pain in her head upon hearing all the things Belladona just said. "That's not true! I didn't kill them. I didn't kill anyone! You. You were the one who killed them, Belladona!" she cried as she held both sides of her head.

"I'm not denying that at all, Angela. I was the one who killed your brother-in-law, Jude. I cut off his manhood that kept on penetrating different holes. And I took out his heart that was never contented with one woman. You should be grateful, Angela, because I helped you! I knew you couldn't do those things all by yourself!"

"Leave now, Belladona! I don't need you, and I don't want to see you ever again! You're the killer, not me!"

As Angela's desperate cries filled the room, Belladona's laughter echoed.

"We're both killers, Angela. Because you are me. I am you. We are one. We were together from the start until now. Through hardships and comfort. Through sadness and happiness. No one gets left behind. Didn't we promise that to each other, huh, Angela? Answer me! Answer me!"

"Please, Belladona, leave... That's enough! That's enough!" Angela cried as her insanity slowly left her. She sat on the floor, shut her eyes tight and covered her ears with her palms. But the sound of Belladona's shrill laugh of triumph still pierced her ears. After a few moments, Angela joined Belladona in laughing. And that was what Andrei saw as he entered the room.

Mystery of the Land of Witchcraft

(An essay on Black magic and Witchcraft in the Mayong village of Assam)

By Debajyoti Gupta, India

We have heard about the witchcraft and black magic or white magic from our school days, there are many stories of black magic in many movies, novels and dramas. The school where young witches are trained in the art of magic in the famous Harry Potter series. But what if I tell you that in India, there's not just a school, but an entire village where black magic isn't just taught—it's a way of life, passed down through generations? Brace yourself, because what you're about to read might leave you utterly horrified!

Welcome to Mayong Village, known as the "Black Magic Capital of India." Here, you might find yourself cured of a serious illness or end up in a worse situation, depending on the magic at play. How can such extreme shifts in fortune occur? In this village, people are said to have strange powers—they can control natural forces, heal the sick, or even cause harm. Curious about how it all works? Let's dive into the mysterious world of magical Mayong Village — The Capital of Black Magic.

Mayong (or Mayang) is a village in Morigaon district, Assam, India. It lies on the bank of the river Brahmaputra, approximately 40 km (25 mi) from the city of Guwahati. Mayong is a tourist attraction because of its history.

Mayong Village has a long history that goes back to ancient times. It was once part of the powerful Ahom kingdom, which ruled Assam for many years.

In the 19th century, Mayong Village came under British colonial rule. The British attempted to suppress the local traditions and beliefs, but the villagers managed to preserve much of their cultural heritage.

The origins of the Mayong Village black magic are unclear. Some say it comes from old tribal rituals, while others think it was influenced by outsiders. It's believed that certain families in the village have secret knowledge and spells passed down through generations, giving Mayong its mysterious reputation.

There are even stories that Mayong is mentioned in the Mahabharata, with some believing that Ghatotkacha got his powers here. Another famous tale is about Muhammad Shah, whose entire army disappeared in the forests around 1330. Despite searches, no trace of the one lakh soldiershas ever been found.

Historian Mirza Mohammad Qasim wrote in the Alamgiri Nama that during the conflict between the Mughals and the Ahom kingdom, the Mughal leader Ram Singh was more afraid of the black magic from Mayong Village than the Ahom army.

Today, the magical Mayong is a thriving village with a diverse population. While the people who practice black magic may be fading from the village, the belief in it remains strong.

While the village's reputation for black magic persists, it has also become a popular tourist destination for curious travelers, history buffs, adventure enthusiasts, and those fascinated by black magic.

Mayong Village Assam is a place full of chilling stories that make you wonder if black magic is real or just a myth. My research revealed something truly terrifying: a journalist who went there found tools with dried blood on them, which some say were used for human or animal sacrifices. Locals have reported seeing people vanish into thin air and witnessing loved ones transform into animals and back again. It's hard to believe, but many people swear it's true.

The locals of Mayong are believed to possess powerful spells that are still effective today. What's even scarier is that if someone shares their problems with a tantrik (a black magic practitioner), the Tantrik might solve the problem in a horrifying way—by ending the person's life instead of just resolving the issue. They believe this is the only way to achieve complete redemption. Spooky, isn't it?

Black magic is no joke! I thought it was all just a myth until I heard the most terrifying story of all. The Beera Cult involves summoning a powerful spirit by highly trained Tantriks only in dire emergencies. If the spells are done wrong, though, instead of the Beera spirit, horrible and malevolent spirits might appear. Just hearing about this kept me awake all night!

These are just a handful of the countless chilling stories I've come across—there are said to be thousands of such tales. However, many people now believe that these frightening practices no longer take place, and visiting the village for a stay is considered completely safe. The thing about Mayong is, the dark arts are not a thing of the past. It is still practiced by some of the residents, and this knowledge will get passed down to generations. Local Assamese folklore has mentions of Mayong and its practice of black magic. Even in Mahabharata, one will find things about Mayong's dark arts. Something to do with Mayong once being the home of *Tantra Kriya*, perhaps?

For those who find the subject of dark arts fascinating, Mayong is gold. No wonder, even with the history of witchcraft, human sacrifice and all things sorcery, Mayong is a very popular tourist destination.

Nowadays, it's said that there isn't much of the old spooky atmosphere left, according to most people. With the world rapidly evolving and people striving to keep up, Mayong Village has shifted from being a haunted place to becoming a significant tourist destination with a dark Mayong village history.

Despite the controversies surrounding black magic practices, the village's rich cultural heritage, natural beauty, and historical significance attract visitors from all over the world.

Yes, you heard that right! They've taken things to the next level, offering tourists a deeper look into the world of black magic. The Mayong Central Museum and Emporium of Black Magic and Witchcraft give a deep look into Mayong's old traditions. Opened by the government in 2002, this museum showcases the village's mystical past and its black magic practices.

Instead of just spooky stories, the museum displays real artifacts related to black magic. You can see ancient manuscripts, skulls, and items used in rituals or sacrifices, showing the villagers' strong belief in witchcraft and sorcery.

Visitors can check out old coins, artificial jewellery, bone and shell bracelets, and metal rings, each with its own story. Live demonstrations on tantra also add to the experience.

Officially known as the "Black Magic Museum in Mayong Village," this museum, with contributions from local families, offers more than just eerie displays. It invites you to consider the reality and impact of witchcraft.

References

1. Mayong Village In Assam: India's Own Hogwarts Of Black Magic, https://wanderon.in/blogs/mayong-village-in-assam

2. Mayong: The land of black magic, witchcraft and necromancy, Times of India, https://timesofindia.indiatimes.com/travel/destinations/mayong-the-land-of-black-magic-witchcraft-and-necromancy/articleshow/91669288.cms

3. Mayong (Assam). Wikipedia. https://en.wikipedia.org/wiki/Mayong_(Assam)

4. "Mayong: A place in Assam where magic 'cures' diseases and helps catch thieves". 27 June 2015.

5. "Mayong: A place in Assam where magic 'cures' diseases and helps catch thieves". *NewsGram*. 27 June 2015.

About the Author

Debajyoti Gupta born in Agartala, Tripura. At present he is research scholar in Tripura University, India.

Sushant Thapa is a Nepalese poet and short story writer with 8 books to his credit. He is a lecturer of English and holds an MA in English Literature from Jawaharlal Nehru University in New Delhi, India.

W.J. Manares, also known as Willer Jun Araneta Manares, is a Filipino author and worldbuilder, primarily associated with the literary scene of Aklan province in the Philippines. He is known for his distinct sardonic and whimsical writing style. Manares is a partner-distributor with Ukiyoto House Philippines and publishes books like "Poets But Us" and "The Arrivers' Earth," according to a Facebook profile and a post on Instagram. He also edits and publishes "Wellerism: magazine of speculatives and shenanigans.

www.ingramcontent.com/pod-product-compliance
Lightning Source LLC
LaVergne TN
LVHW041846070526
838199LV00045BA/1464